The
Illustrated Treasury
of
FAIRY
TALES

The Illustrated Treasury of FAIRY TALES

Edited by T.A. Kennedy

*Art Direction and Book Design
by Natalie Provenzano*

HODDER AND STOUGHTON
LONDON SYDNEY AUCKLAND TORONTO

The Illustrated treasury of fairy tales.
   1. Tales   2. Legends
   I. Kennedy, T.A.
   398.2   PZ8.1

   ISBN 0-340-35367-8

First published 1982 by Grosset and Dunlap, Inc. New York
First published in Great Britain in 1984

Published by Hodder and Stoughton Children's Books,
a division of Hodder and Stoughton Ltd, Mill Road,
Dunton Green, Sevenoaks, Kent TN13 2YJ

Printed in Belgium by Henri Proost & Cie, Turnhout

*Grateful acknowledgement is made to Doug Cushman for permission to reprint
illustrations from Giants © 1980 by Doug Cushman.*

Contents

The Steadfast Tin Soldier   11

Jack and the Beanstalk   17

Cinderella   24

Puss in Boots   32

The Twelve Dancing Princesses   38

Snow White and the Seven Dwarfs   46

Diamonds and Toads   52

The Snow Queen   57

The Three Sillies   101

Beauty and the Beast   111

The Golden Goose   135

Rumpelstiltskin   140

The Sleeping Beauty in the Wood   147

The Princess and the Pea   155

Rapunzel   158

The Sorcerer's Apprentice   166

Red Riding Hood   171

The Bremen Town Musicians   177

Snow–white and Rose–red   185

List of Illustrators

Anthony Accardo, 101–105, 107–109, 135, 137–141

Doug Cushman, 19, 20, 22–23, 191

Betsy Day, 11, 13, 15, 17, 47, 51, 53–56, 156, 157, 168, 169

Eulalie, 32, 33, 35–37, 149–151, 154, 171, 173–176

John B. Gruelle, 24–31

George and Doris Hauman, 177–183

M.L. Kirk, 170

Karen Milone, 39–42, 45, 111–113, 115, 116, 118, 120–122, 124–125, 127, 128, 130–133, 158–161, 163–165

Kathy Mitchell, 58, 59, 61–63, 65, 67–69, 73, 74, 76–80, 82–86, 88, 91–93, 95–98, 100

Jessie Willcox Smith, 48, 153, 184

Tasha Tudor, 155, 167

Cover illustration by Ponder Goembel
Back cover illustration by Eulalie

Introduction

A fairy tale, like any other classic, is something that endures. It comes alive over and over again for each new generation of readers to enjoy. And so it is a special privilege to be able to offer a collection that, in many ways, draws those generations together.

This is a unique collection, for it includes the work of a succession of classic illustrators, each of whom offers an extraordinary vision of a fairy tale world. It is almost as if the reader is allowed to travel through time—from the nostalgic, porcelain figures of artist Jessie Wilcox Smith, through the whimsical lines of Eulalie and the startled innocence of John B. Gruelle—all the way to the drama of Karen Milone's "Rapunzel" and the colourful comedy of Doug Cushman's "Jack and the Beanstalk."

And so each tale, told in pictures, comes alive again, each to be treasured as they have been treasured before. And yet, whether the stories and illustrations in this book come out of the past or from the present—each will be made brand new by the eyes of a child.

And whether or not these tales are familiar, or the pictures those that have been seen before, they will come alive again through the children, to be enjoyed by us all. For a fairy tale is a chance for everyone to believe in magic. To travel to that special place where pumpkins turn to golden coaches, and frogs to princes; and where everyone lives happily ever after—after all. It is a chance to believe—if only for a little while—in the faraway world of once upon a time.

T.A. Kennedy

The Steadfast
Tin Soldier

THERE were once twenty-five tin soldiers who were all brothers, for they were all born of the same tin spoon. They carried their muskets on their shoulders and looked straight in front of them; their uniform was red and blue, and very pretty indeed. The very first thing they heard in the world, when the lid was lifted off the box were the words, "Tin soldiers!" for that is what a little boy cried, clapping his hands, as he saw them. They were given to him because it was his birthday, and one by one, he set them up on the table.

All the soldiers were just alike except one, who was a little different. He had only one leg, for he was the last to be cast and there was not enough tin. But he stood just as steadily on his one leg as the others stood on their two. And it was just this one who became famous.

11

On the table where they were all set up, there also stood a beautiful castle made of cardboard. Through the small windows you could see straight into the rooms; little trees were standing outside around a little bit of mirror that represented a lake. Swans made of wax were swimming there, and reflected in the glass. This was very pretty; but the prettiest thing of all was a little maid who was standing at the open door of the castle. She was also cut out of cardboard, but she wore a skirt of the finest gauze, and a little narrow blue ribbon like a sash, in the middle of which there was a bit of glittering tinsel as large as her whole face. The little maid stretched out both her arms, for she was a dancer, and she lifted one of her legs so high that the Tin Soldier could not see it at all, and thought that she had only one leg like himself.

"That would be the wife for me," he thought, "but she is so aristocratic, and lives in a castle. I have only a box that belongs to the whole twenty-five of us. I know that is no place for her, but I would like to make her acquaintance just the same." So he went and stood behind a snuffbox where he could watch the little maid, who kept standing on one leg all the time without losing her balance.

Toward evening all the other soldiers were put into the box, and the people in the house went to bed. Then the toys began to play, coming alive one by one. They paid visits and went to war, and gave parties and dances. The tin soldiers rattled in their box, for they wanted to join in the fun too, but they could not get the lid off. The nutcrackers were turning somersaults; the slate pencil was at work on the slate; and there was such a noise that the canary woke up and began to join in the chatter. The only two who did not move from their places were the Tin Soldier and the little dancer. She was standing straight up on the tip of her toe, with both arms stretched out, and the Tin Soldier stood just as firmly on his one leg, unable to take his eyes off her, even for a moment.

The clock struck twelve when, bang! Off went the lid of the snuff-box. There was no snuff in it, but only a tiny black goblin, and a clever little goblin it was. "Tin Soldier," said the goblin, "please keep your eyes to yourself." But the Tin Soldier just pretended not to hear. "Well," said the goblin, "you just wait till tomorrow."

When the children of the house came down in the morning, the Tin Soldier was put on the windowsill. And whether it was the goblin or the draught that did it, all of a sudden the window flew up, and the soldier fell head over heels from the third storey. He came down at a terrible rate, and got stuck by his helmet, with his leg sticking straight up in the air, and his bayonet between the paving stones. The children went down to look for him, but even though they nearly stepped on him, they could not see him, and gave up and went back inside.

If only the little Tin Soldier had cried, "Here I am!" perhaps they might have found him, but he did not think it proper to call out loudly when he was in uniform.

Then it began to rain; the drops fell thicker and thicker until it became a real downpour. When it was over, two street boys came along. "Look," they cried, "here's a tin soldier! Let's send him for a sail!" So they made a little boat of newspaper, put the Tin Soldier inside, and there he was, sailing down the gutter. The two boys ran alongside and clapped their hands. Goodness! What large waves were in that gutter, and how strong the current was! But then, it had been a real downpour.

The paper boat was tossed up and down, now and then it turned round and round until the poor Tin Soldier was quite dizzy. But he was very brave and didn't move a muscle; he just looked straight in front of him and shouldered his musket. Then, all at once the boat drifted into a long drain pipe, where it was just as dark as if he had been in his box. "Where am I going now?" he thought. "All this must surely be the goblin's fault. But, if the little lady dancer were here in the boat with me, I would not mind if it were twice as dark." And he sighed to himself and wondered if he would ever see her again.

Suddenly they came upon a huge water rat who lived in the drain pipe. "Have you a passport?" asked the rat. The Tin Soldier said not a word, and held his musket tighter than ever. Away went the boat, and the rat after it, gnashing his teeth and calling out: "Stop him, stop him! He hasn't got a passport, he hasn't paid the toll!" But the current grew stronger and stronger, and before long, the Tin Soldier could see daylight down at the end of the pipe. Then he heard a great roaring sound, which would have frightened the boldest, for just where the gutter ended, the water poured out into a large canal. And it was just as dangerous for the Tin Soldier as it is for anyone to be carried over a waterfall.

He was so near it that he could not stop, and so the little paper boat was swept into the canal. The poor Tin Soldier stiffened himself as well as he could, and no one could say that he even batted an eyelid. The boat whirled around and around, filled up with water, and began to sink. The Tin Soldier stood up to his neck in water, and the boat sank deeper, and at last the water came up over his head. The Soldier thought only of the little dancer with her outstretched arms, and of how he would never see her again.

The paper boat burst, and the Tin Soldier fell through the drain, where he was at once gobbled up by a great fish. Oh! how dark it was in there, even worse than in the drainpipe, and there was so little room. But the Tin Soldier was very brave, and lay down full length with his musket on his shoulder. The fish darted about in the most alarming way, not at all sure what he had swallowed, and then for a time it lay quite still. Suddenly there was a flash like lightning! Daylight appeared, and he heard someone cry, "Tin Soldier!" The fish had been caught, taken to the market and sold, and brought to the kitchen, where the cook cut it up with a big knife. She took the Tin Soldier by her two fingers and marched him into the sitting room, where they all wanted to see the remarkable man who had been travelling about in the inside of a fish. For himself, the Tin Soldier wasn't at all proud. But when they stood him on the table—well! What curious things happen in the world! He found that he was in the exact same room as he had been before. He saw the same children, the same castle, and most important of all—there was the little dancer, still standing on one leg with the other high in the air, and her arms outstretched to him. She looked so brave and beautiful that the Tin Soldier was almost ready to weep tin tears, but of course that would not have been at all proper. He looked at her, and she at him, but they said nothing. Then, all at once, one of the little boys took up the Tin Soldier and threw him into the fireplace without any reason at all. It must have been the fault of the goblin in the snuff-box, who was terribly jealous of the soldier's return. The Tin Soldier was quite lit up, and felt a great heat, but he still gazed upon the little dancer, and whether it was from fire or from love, he could not tell.

Before long, his colours were gone, but whether it happened from the heat or from grief no one could say. He looked at the little maiden and she at him; he felt that he was melting, but he stood there bravely and shouldered his musket. Suddenly, the door flew open, and a draught caught the dancer and she flew straight into the fireplace with the Tin Soldier, blazed up in a flame and was gone. The Tin Soldier melted into a lump, and when the servant maid came to clean the ashes the next day, all she found was a little tin heart. Of the dancer nothing was left but the small bit of tinsel that was burnt as black as a cinder.

Jack and
the Beanstalk

A LONG time ago, when the world was young and folk did what they liked, there lived a boy named Jack. Jack was the only son of a poor widow who could barely scrape together enough to make an evening meal. They had but a scrawny cow to give them milk and butter and, alas, soon even that was sour. Since the old cow became such a burden to feed, Jack's mother decided there was no recourse but to sell her.

"I know this cow is thin and gives little milk," Jack's mother told him, "but she should still bring in enough money for us to buy some food. Go to the marketplace, son, and do your best."

Now, Jack was a good and loving son, but he was not all that clever. As he walked along the road to the marketplace, he tried to console himself by thinking of all the things he could buy with the money he would get for the cow. He imagined he could get ten, or fifty, or maybe even one hundred gold pieces for old Bessie.

By and by, he met an old man. Jack tipped his hat and thought it a bit odd when the stranger called out, "Good morning, Jack." But, then again, there were plenty of Jacks in this part of the country, so Jack paid little attention.

"Good morning," replied Jack.

"And where may you be going?" asked the strange man.

"I'm off to the market to sell my cow," Jack explained, feeling very grown-up and important.

"Then look what I have here, Jack. Something that would make your mother very proud of you." And the old man held out his hand, showing Jack five round beans. "I'll trade these magic beans for your old cow. If you plant them overnight, by morning they will have grown right up into the sky."

Jack thought the beans were delightful, and the old man seemed wise and honest, so the trade was made. As Jack hurried off, he heard the old man call after him, "You'll need your courage, Jack, to free the harp and hen. But with gold as your reward, you'll ne'er be poor again." Jack paid little attention, eager as he was to show his mother what a good trade he had made for the cow.

When Jack returned home, his mother was waiting anxiously for him at the gate. "I see you have sold the cow," she called out happily. "Tell me what you were able to get for her."

Jack held out the beans triumphantly, and his mother was furious. She sent Jack directly to bed without a scrap to eat, which was easy to do considering they had nothing to eat that night, anyway. Then she threw the beans right out of the window.

The next morning, when Jack awakened, a dark green light shone in his room. The little window was covered with a curtain of leaves. As he looked out, he saw the tallest beanstalk he had ever seen, the top so high, it disappeared into the morning clouds.

Well, since there was no cow to milk, and no butter to churn, Jack decided he would climb the giant beanstalk. So he climbed and he climbed. It was easy work, for the big beanstalk with the leaves growing out of each side was like a ladder. Jack rested only twice, and by noontime, he had reached the top. Poking his head through the clouds, he looked about.

In the distance was a huge castle. Jack was hungry from his long climb and hoped that maybe in the castle he could get some food. But just as he reached the huge door, he heard a thundering sound so loud it shook Jack off his feet. He barely had time to slip into a crack in the pavement, when an enormous giant strode right over him. As the giant opened the great door, Jack scampered in after him. He hid behind some firewood and cautiously looked around the room.

Jack found himself right in the middle of a huge kitchen where the giant's wife was cooking lunch in a giant cauldron. The giant himself was seated at the table with three large bags of gold pieces in front of him. He started counting each piece of gold and, as he reached five hundred and eighty-six, the giant stuck his nose up in the air and sniffed. Suddenly he roared:

"*Fee-fi-fo-fum,*
I smell the blood of an Englishman.
Be he alive, or be he dead,
I'll grind his bones to make my bread."

"Really!" said the giant's wife. "You're only smelling the Englishman you ate last night." And she handed him his meal. They both ate in silence.

When they had finished, the giant roared, "Bring me my hen that lays the golden eggs."

So the wife brought him a great black hen with a shining red comb. Then she went about her business clearing the luncheon dishes.

Suddenly the giant roared, "Lay!" and the black hen promptly laid— not an ordinary egg—a beautiful, shiny, golden egg!

Jack could hardly believe his eyes. But soon the giant had ordered up a whole basketful of golden eggs, and he became tired of playing with his hen.

Next, the giant rose and went to the closet. He removed a beautiful golden harp and placed it on the table. When he yelled "Sing!" the harp began a lovely tune. The singing lasted for most of an hour, and when it stopped, both the giant and his wife were fast asleep.

Remembering the riddle of the strange old man, Jack slipped out from behind the firewood, climbed up to the top of the table, and tied together the three bags of gold. These he slung over his back and, with his other arm, grabbed the hen that laid the golden eggs, and then the harp. He slid down the tablecloth, racing across the floor.

But just as Jack reached the door, the harp began to call out, awakening the giant. Running as fast as he could, Jack reached the beanstalk and climbed down, but the giant was close behind.

As soon as he was safely to the ground, Jack grabbed an ax from the woodpile and chopped away at the beanstalk. At long last, the stalk tumbled down, and down came the angry giant as well. The giant hit the ground so hard that he left a hole that was one hundred feet wide and two hundred feet deep.

Years later the hole had filled with water from rain, and Jack and his mother had the finest lake you could imagine. With the money from the gold, they had built a beautiful house next to the lake, and the hen ran free, and the magic harp played beautiful music. And so they lived for many years and never wanted for anything for the rest of their lives.

Cinderella

ONCE upon a time there lived a man who took for his second wife the most disagreeable woman that ever lived. She had two daughters who were both exactly like herself, and the man likewise had a daughter. But unlike the others, this girl was sweet and good and kind, as well as being more beautiful than any of them.

The girl's stepmother was very jealous of her, for all of her good qualities made her own daughters the more hateful by comparison. And so the mother and her daughters came to treat the poor girl very badly, setting her to the roughest housework from dawn till dark. Her only bed was in a corner of the hearth amongst the ashes. And it was for this reason that she came to be called Cinderella.

But the girl suffered all in silence, wearing the shabbiest clothes, and working until she was too tired to stand.

It happened that the King's son was to give a great ball, and all the young ladies of the kingdom were to be invited. Cinderella's stepsisters were so excited at the invitation that they could talk of nothing else—and spent their whole time deciding what to wear.

"I," said the elder of them, "shall wear my velvet gown with trimmings of the finest lace."

"And I," said the younger, "shall wear the silk and brocade, and put on my diamond tiara. Then we shall see who is the more splendid."

Then the elder sister grew angry, and the two began to fuss and fight until Cinderella sought to intervene. She gave them the best advice she could, and offered to dress them herself, that there might be none more perfectly decked out than they.

At last the long-awaited evening came, and Cinderella dressed them each so splendidly that even the sisters could not decide who was the more beautiful.

While poor Cinderella was arranging the last of the details, the elder sister said teasingly, "Cinderella, do you not wish to go to the ball?" And the wicked sisters began to laugh at the girl until she thought her heart would break.

When they had gone, poor Cinderella sat down in her corner of the hearth and cried and cried. Immediately a Fairy Godmother appeared and asked, "What are you weeping for, little maid?"

"Oh," sighed Cinderella, "I wish—I wish—." But she sobbed so hard that she could not get the words out.

"You wish to go to the ball, isn't it so?"

Cinderella nodded.

"Well, then be a good girl, and I will see to it that you shall go. First, run into the garden and fetch me a pumpkin. Get a good one now—the largest one there is."

Cinderella did not understand, but went and did as she was told. The Godmother took the pumpkin, and with one touch of her magic wand, it became a splendid gilt coach, lined with satin. Cinderella could hardly believe her eyes.

"Now, fetch me the mouse trap out of the kitchen, my dear."

Cinderella brought it, and found that it held six fat, sleek mice. The Fairy struck each of them with the wand, and each became a beautiful black horse, prancing about the courtyard.

"You will need coachmen, Cinderella—what shall I do for them?"

Cinderella thought that a rat from the rat trap might do, and ran to bring it to her Fairy Godmother. Instantly he was changed into a splendid coachman with the finest whiskers imaginable. The Godmother then took six lizards from the garden, and they were changed into six footmen, all splendidly dressed, who immediately jumped up on the carriage as though they had been footmen all of their days.

"Well, Cinderella, now you can go to the ball."

"Oh, Godmother! You are very kind, but how can I go, dressed like this?"

The Fairy only laughed, and touched her with the wand. All at once her wretched rags became the most splendid gown imaginable, threaded with silver and gold, and studded with jewels. The skirt was lengthened to a train of sweeping satin, and underneath it, out peeped her little feet, covered in silk stockings and adorned with the prettiest glass slippers in the world.

"Now, Cinderella, you may go, but remember this: If you stay one minute past midnight, all will be as it was. Your coach will be a pumpkin, your footmen lizards, your coachman a rat, and the horses mice. Even you will change back to the cinder–wench you were."

Cinderella promised she would return in time, and drove off into the night.

She drew up to the palace gates where the Prince himself awaited her. He offered her his hand, and led her to the ballroom, where all assembled stood aside to let the couple pass, and whispered among themselves as to who she might be. Everyone agreed that they had never seen anyone so beautiful.

The Prince himself would dance with no one else, and could not take his eyes off her.

In fact, the two were so taken with one another that the time slipped by unnoticed, and all at once, Cinderella realized with horror that the clock had begun to strike twelve. She jumped up and ran from the ballroom as lightly as a deer. The Prince tried to follow her, but by the time he reached the palace gate, all he saw was a dirty cinder–wench outside, holding a pumpkin. The beautiful lady had vanished.

He came back to the ballroom, saddened and weary, and found to his joy that the beautiful lady had dropped one of her glass slippers on the stair. He took it up and put it in his pocket.

Meanwhile, Cinderella arrived back home, cold and weary, without coach, or coachman or horses, and sat herself in her usual place by the hearth. All she had left of the wonderful evening was one of the little glass slippers, which, for some reason, had not disappeared with all the rest.

When her stepsisters returned from the ball, they were full of stories about the mysterious lady, and how, at the stroke of midnight she had jumped up and run from the palace, dropping one of her slippers on the way. No one knew who she was, or where she had gone. And the Prince, the sisters told her, looked to everyone as though he had fallen deeply in love.

Cinderella listened to all this in silence, turning her face to the fire so that they would think it was just the heat that made her cheeks so rosy and her eyes so bright. And the next morning she returned to her weary work just as before.

Before three days had passed, the whole town was astir with the news that the Prince had ordered that every lady in the kingdom was to try on a little glass slipper, in hopes that he might find the one who had come to the ball. Princesses and duchesses, and gentlewomen of all kinds tried their best to fit the slipper, but as it was a fairy slipper none could get it to fit. And besides, no one could produce the fellow-slipper, which all the time lay in the pocket of Cinderella's old woollen dress.

At last the Prince came to the house of the two sisters, and though they knew well enough that it was neither of them who had worn the slipper, they tried their best to fit into it anyway. They each pushed and pulled at it, and tried to squeeze their clumsy feet into it until tears came to their eyes, but to no avail.

"Let me try it," Cinderella called from her corner by the hearth.

"You?" cried the others. They shouted with laughter, but as the Prince had ordered that every maiden in the city should try it on, they had to agree. So the Prince bade Cinderella to sit and try it on, and lo and behold, it fitted exactly. And before anyone could speak she drew the other slipper from her pocket and put it on as well. And with the touch of the magic slippers, she was all at once changed into the beautiful lady who had been at the ball.

The Prince took her in his arms and kissed her. And the wicked sisters, who recognized what had happened, threw themselves at her feet and begged her forgiveness for being so spiteful and mean.

Cinderella related the whole tale, and all were so taken with her beauty and grace that they fell in love with her all over again. And the Prince was so delighted to have found his love again that he insisted on marrying her that very day. Cinderella never went home again, and never had to sit by the hearth, but she sent for her two stepsisters and married them to members of the court. And as far as anyone knows, they all lived happily ever after.

Puss In Boots

ONCE there was a miller whose sole worldly possessions were his mill, his ass, and his cat. That was all he had to leave his three sons upon his death. So he called in no lawyer and made no will, but simply left the mill to the eldest, the ass to the second, and the cat to the youngest.

The youngest son was quite downcast about his inheritance. "My brothers," he said to himself, "by putting their goods together will be able to earn an honest livelihood. But once I have eaten my cat and sold his skin, I shall have nothing."

Puss, who was sitting quietly on the window seat, overheard these words. Looking up, he said with a very serious, sober air, "Please, dear master, do not worry about your future. Only give me a bag and a pair of boots, so that I may stride through the brambles, and you will soon see that you have a better bargain than you think."

As soon as Puss was provided with what he had asked for, he drew on his boots and, slinging the bag round his neck, took hold of the two strings with his fore-paws. Then he set off for a warren he knew was stocked with rabbits. There he filled his bag with bran and weeds, stretched himself out as stiffly as though he were dead, and waited patiently till some simple young rabbit, unused to worldly snares and wiles, should see the dainty feast. He had lain scarcely a few moments, before a thoughtless young rabbit caught at the bait and went headlong into the bag. Immediately, the cat drew the strings and strangled the foolish creature.

Puss was vastly proud of his victory. He went straight to the palace to see the King. When he was shown into the King's cabinet, he bowed respectfully to His Majesty and said, "Sire, I bring you a rabbit from the warren of the Marquis of Carabas." (Such was the title the cat took it into his head to give his master.)

"Tell your master that I am obliged by his courtesy, and that I accept his present with much pleasure," replied the King.

Later Puss went and hid himself in a cornfield, and held his bag open as before. Soon two partridges were lured into the trap. Puss quickly drew the strings and made them both prisoners. He then went and presented them to the King, as he had done the rabbit. The King received the partridges very graciously, and ordered the messenger to be rewarded for his trouble. For two or three months, Puss continued to carry game to the King, always presenting it in the name of his master, the Marquis of Carabas.

One day Puss happened to hear that the King was going to take a drive along the bank of the river, accompanied by his daughter, the most beautiful princess in the world. He said to his master, "If you follow my advice, your fortune will be as good as made. You need only go and bathe in the river at the spot that I shall point out, and leave the rest to me."

The Marquis did as his cat advised. As he was bathing, the King came driving past. Puss began to bawl as loudly as he could, "Help! Help! The Marquis of Carabas is drowning!"

On hearing this, the King looked out of the carriage window. Recognizing the cat who had so often brought him game, he ordered his bodyguard to fly to the assistance of the Marquis of Carabas.

While the poor Marquis was being fished out of the river, Puss stepped up to the royal carriage. He told His Majesty that during the time his master was bathing, some robbers had stolen his clothes. Puss, of course, had hidden them under a large stone. The King immediately ordered the gentlemen of his wardrobe to go and fetch one of his most sumptuous dresses for the Marquis of Carabas.

When the Marquis, who was a handsome young fellow, came forth gaily dressed, he looked so elegant that the King took him for a very fine gentleman, and the Princess fell head over heels in love with him. The King insisted on his getting into the carriage and taking a drive with them.

Puss, highly delighted at the turn things were taking, and determined that all should turn out in the very best way, now ran on before the carriage. When he reached a meadow where some peasants were mowing the grass, he hurried up to them. "I say, good folk," he cried, "if you do not tell the King, when he comes this way, that the field you are mowing belongs to the Marquis of Carabas, you shall all be chopped to bits."

When the carriage passed by, the King put his head out and asked the mowers whose good grassland that was. "It belongs to the Marquis of Carabas, please Your Majesty," said they breathlessly, for the cat's threats had frightened them mightily.

"Upon my word, Marquis," said the King, "that is a fine estate you have."

"Yes, sire," replied the Marquis with an easy air. "It yields me a tolerable income every year."

Puss, who continued to run on before the carriage, presently came up to some reapers. "I say, you reapers," cried he, "mind you tell the King that this corn belongs to the Marquis of Carabas, or else you shall all be chopped into mincemeat."

The King passed by a moment after and inquired to whom those cornfields belonged. "To the Marquis of Carabas, please Your Majesty," replied the reapers.

"Faith, it pleases me right well to see the beloved Marquis is so wealthy!" said the King.

Puss kept running on before the carriage and repeating the same instructions to all the labourers he met, and the King was astounded at the vast possessions of the Marquis of Carabas. He kept congratulating the Marquis, while the newly-made nobleman received each fresh compliment more lightly than the last, so that one could see he really was a Marquis, and a very grand one, too.

At length Puss reached a magnificent castle belonging to an ogre, who was immensely rich, since all the lands the King had been riding through were a portion of his estate. Puss inquired what sort of a person the ogre might be, and what he was able to do. Then he sent in a message asking leave to speak with the ogre, adding that he was unwilling to pass so near his castle without paying his respects to him.

The ogre received Puss as civilly as it is in the nature of an ogre to do. "I have been told," said Puss, "that you have the power of transforming yourself into all sorts of animals, such as a lion or an elephant."

"So I have," replied the ogre sharply. "Do you doubt it? Look, and you shall see me become a lion at once."

When Puss suddenly saw a lion before him, he was seized with such a fright that he scrambled up to the roof, although it was no easy job, owing to his boots. When the ogre had returned to his natural shape, Puss came down again and confessed he had been exceedingly frightened.

"I have also been told," added Puss, "only I really cannot believe it, that you likewise possess the power of taking the shape of the smallest animals, and that you could change yourself into a rat or a mouse. But that is surely impossible."

"Impossible, indeed!" cried the ogre. "You shall see."

So saying, the ogre took on the shape of a mouse, and began frisking about on the ground. Puss immediately pounced upon him, gave him one shake, and put an end to him.

By this time the King had reached the gates of the ogre's magnificent castle. Puss, hearing the rumbling of the carriage across the drawbridge, ran out to meet the King, crying, "Your Majesty is welcome to the castle of the Marquis of Carabas."

"What! My dear Marquis," exclaimed the King, "does this castle also belong to you? Really, I never saw anything more splendid than the courtyard and the surrounding buildings. Pray let us see if the inside is equal to the outside."

The Marquis gracefully helped the Princess out of the carriage. Following the King, they mounted a flight of steps and were ushered by Puss into a vast hall, where they found an elegant feast spread. Some of the ogre's friends were to have visited him that day, but the news had spread that the King was about, and they dared not come.

The King was positively delighted. The castle was magnificent, and the Marquis of Carabas was such an excellent young man. Furthermore, the Princess was clearly in love with him. So, after drinking five or six glasses of wine, His Majesty hemmed and hawed and then said, "You have only to say the word, Marquis, to become my son-in-law."

The Marquis bowed and looked tenderly at the Princess. That very day they were married. Puss, who had brought it all about, looked on, mightily pleased. And ever afterward he lived in the castle as a great lord, and hunted mice for mere sport whenever he pleased.

The Twelve
Dancing Princesses

ONCE upon a time there was a King who had twelve daughters, each more beautiful than the last. They slept together in a hall where their beds were lined in two rows on either side. At night, when the Princesses had gone to bed, the King would lock and bolt the door. But when he unlocked it in the morning, he found that their slippers had been danced to pieces, and no one could explain how it happened.

So the King sent out a proclamation, saying that whoever could discover his daughters' secret might choose one of the Princesses for his wife, and inherit half the kingdom. But if, after three days, whoever should try failed to discover where they did their night's dancing, he would be banished from the kingdom for the rest of his days.

It came to pass that a Prince soon appeared and offered to take the risk. He was happily received, and that night was taken to a little chamber adjoining the one where the Princesses slept. His bed was made up there, and he was to watch the whole night through and find out where it was that they went to dance. The door to his room was left open so that none could leave without being seen. But after a long while, the Prince's eyes grew heavy and he fell fast asleep. When he woke in the morning, all the Princesses had once again been dancing, for their shoes were full of holes.

And so it was for the second and third nights. And though the unfortunate Prince pleaded with the King, he was granted no mercy and was banished from the land for the rest of his days. And it was just the same with all the other young men who came after him. They too, were banished from the kingdom.

Now it happened that a poor soldier found himself on the road to the town where the King lived. He fell in with an old woman who asked him where he was going.

"I really don't know myself," answered the soldier. And he added in fun: "But if the truth be known, I should really like to discover where it is that the Princesses do their night's dancing, and after that I think I should like to become King."

"That really is not so difficult," said the old woman. "Do not drink the wine which is brought to you before you retire in the evening, but nonetheless, you must pretend that you have fallen fast asleep." Then she handed him a short cloak, saying; "When you wear this you will be invisible, in order that you may follow the Princesses where they go."

When the soldier heard this good advice he considered the matter more seriously, and decided to go to the palace and try his luck. He appeared before the King, was as happily received as the others, and dressed in the most splendid of royal garments.

That night, when bedtime came, he was conducted to the chamber. As he was about to go to bed, the eldest Princess appeared and offered him a glass of wine. She waited to see him drink, but the clever soldier had fastened a sponge under his chin, and let all the wine run down into it, so that he did not drink so much as a drop. Then he lay himself down and snored, pretending to be in the deepest sleep.

The twelve in the next room heard him and laughed. The eldest said: "Too bad, he too must be banished." And with that they rose from their beds, went to their closets and cupboards, and brought out their beautiful ball gowns. They decked themselves out as grandly as possible, skipping and giggling while they admired themselves before the mirrors.

Only the youngest sister said: "I don't know what it is, but I feel so strange. Some misfortune is certainly hanging over us."

"You are a goose," said the eldest. "You are always frightened about something. Have you forgotten how many princes have come here in vain? Why, I didn't even need to give that clumsy soldier a sleeping potion—he never would have awakened at all!"

When they were all ready, they peeped in at the soldier, but his eyes were tightly shut and he did not stir. So, thinking they were all quite safe, the eldest went up and knocked on one of the beds. It sank right into the earth and, one by one, they each descended after it.

The soldier, who had seen everything, quickly threw on his cloak and went down behind the youngest. Halfway down, he trod on her dress.

She was startled, and cried aloud: "What was that? Who has hold of my dress?"

"Don't be a ninny," the eldest sister scolded her, "you must have caught it on a nail."

They continued down, and when they got quite underground they stood on a beautiful avenue, lined with trees. All the leaves were silver, and glittered and shone.

The soldier thought, "I must take some proof of where I've been." But when he broke off a twig, there was a sharp crack.

The youngest Princess cried out again, "All is not well! Did you hear that?"

"Those are just salutes from this place because we have once again eluded our 'Prince'!" the eldest answered her.

The whole procession of them turned a corner and came to another avenue where the leaves of the trees were made of gold, and at last to a third where they were made of glittering diamonds. From each of these the soldier took a twig, and each time there was a crack that made the youngest Princess start with terror. Yet the eldest insisted that these were only triumphal salutes. They came to a great lake then, and close to the bank were tied twelve little boats. In each of them sat a handsome Prince, waiting for his Princess. Each took her place in one of the boats, but the soldier seated himself next to the youngest.

And her Prince began to row. After a time he said, "I can't imagine why, but the boat is strangely heavy today. I have to row with all my strength just to get it along."

"I wonder why it is," said the Princess, "unless perhaps it is the hot weather. Does it not seem strangely hot to you?"

43

Across the lake was a brilliantly lighted castle and they could hear the strains of a great orchestra tuning up for the dancing with the joyous music of trumpets and drums. They reached the shore and every Prince began to dance with his beloved. And the soldier joined the party too, unseen. If someone held out a cup of wine, he drank it, so that it was empty when lifted to the lips. The youngest one was frightened at this, but the eldest always bade her hush and not be foolish.

They danced until three in the morning, when their shoes were danced to shreds and they were all obliged to stop. This time the soldier took his seat next to the eldest Princess while the Princes rowed them all back across the lake. On the bank they kissed goodbye, and promised to come again the next evening.

When they reached the staircase to the world above, the soldier ran on ahead of them and lay down in bed. And when the twelve began to straggle in, slowly and wearily, he began to snore very loudly, so that they said: "Well, we are certainly safe as far as he is concerned." Then they took off their beautiful dresses, put them away, and placed the worn out dancing slippers under their beds.

The next morning the soldier had resolved to say nothing, so that he might go with them and see the wonderful doings again.

So he went along for two more nights, having a time dancing and drinking their wine. The last night, he was even so bold as to take along a wine goblet as a token.

The next day, the appointed hour for his answer came, and he went to the King with all of his proof. The twelve Princesses all stood outside the door, giggling at what they thought would be his answer.

The King put the question: "Where is it that my daughters go to dance their shoes to pieces?" And the soldier answered. "They dance with twelve Princes in an underground castle. See? I have brought you my proof, a twig of silver, one of gold, and the last of diamonds. Here is also a goblet that I have brought with me from the castle."

Thereupon the King sent for his daughters, who, being not far away, tumbled in from outside the doorway and into his chambers, where the soldier stood smiling. Seeing that they were found out at last, and that it would do no good to deny the matter, they confessed everything.

Then the King asked the soldier which of the Princesses he would choose for his wife.

"I would have the cleverest of them," he said. "Your youngest daughter is the one I choose."

And so he was wed to the youngest Princess, and given half the kingdom to rule. And as for the rest of them, their Princes were enchanted, and for every night they had stolen away to dance, they added a day to their sweethearts' enchantment, and were obliged to wait until it was over.

Snow White and the Seven Dwarfs

ON a winter's day many years ago, a Queen sat sewing at her palace window. Through the window, framed in black ebony, she saw the gleaming white snow.

Suddenly the Queen pricked her finger, and three tiny drops of blood appeared.

"I wish I had a baby," thought the Queen, "with skin as white as this snow, lips as red as this blood, and hair as black as the ebony of the window frame."

Soon afterwards her wish came true. A lovely little daughter was born to the Queen. She had skin as white as snow, lips as red as blood, and hair as black as ebony. She was named Snow White.

A few years later the Queen died, and the King married again. The new Queen was very proud and vain. She thought herself the most beautiful woman in the world. She had a magic mirror, and every day she would look into it and ask,

"Magic mirror on the wall,
Who is the fairest of us all?"

And the mirror would reply,

"Thou art the fairest, Lady Queen."

But as Snow White grew up, she became more and more lovely. Soon she was even more beautiful than the Queen, her stepmother.

One day the Queen stood as usual before her mirror, and asked,

"Magic mirror on the wall,
Who is the fairest of us all?"

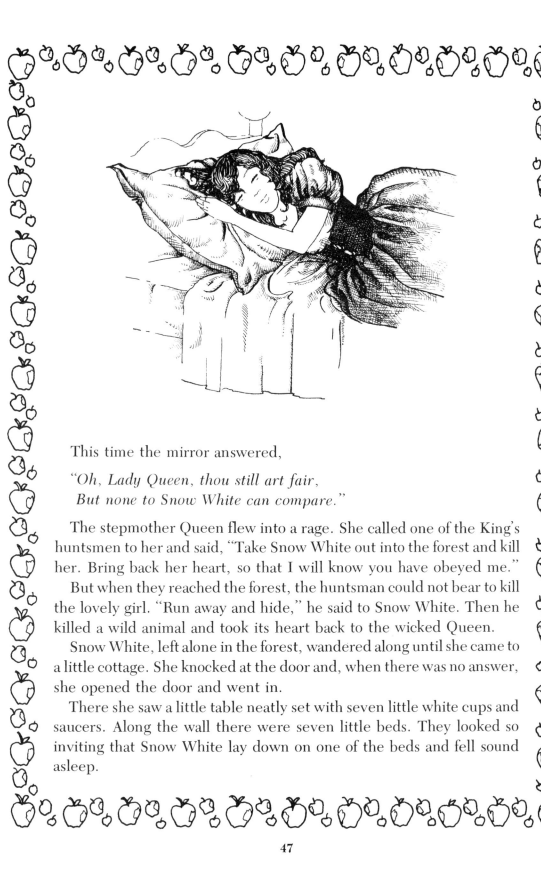

This time the mirror answered,

"Oh, Lady Queen, thou still art fair,
But none to Snow White can compare."

The stepmother Queen flew into a rage. She called one of the King's huntsmen to her and said, "Take Snow White out into the forest and kill her. Bring back her heart, so that I will know you have obeyed me."

But when they reached the forest, the huntsman could not bear to kill the lovely girl. "Run away and hide," he said to Snow White. Then he killed a wild animal and took its heart back to the wicked Queen.

Snow White, left alone in the forest, wandered along until she came to a little cottage. She knocked at the door and, when there was no answer, she opened the door and went in.

There she saw a little table neatly set with seven little white cups and saucers. Along the wall there were seven little beds. They looked so inviting that Snow White lay down on one of the beds and fell sound asleep.

This was the home of the Seven Dwarfs, and soon they returned from the mountains. When they lit the candles, they saw Snow White asleep on the bed. "How beautiful she is," they said softly, so as not to disturb her. And they let her sleep there until morning.

The next day the Seven Dwarfs crowded around Snow White. "Who are you?" they asked. "How did you get here?"

Snow White told the Dwarfs about her wicked stepmother, and how the huntsman had spared her life. "Now I am without a home," she said.

"Would you like to live with us?" asked the Dwarfs. "You could sew and mend, and keep everything tidy."

This made Snow White very happy. "Oh, thank you," she said. "I could want nothing better." So she stayed and took care of the home of the Seven Dwarfs.

Off in the palace, the stepmother thought that Snow White was dead. But one day she went to her mirror as usual and asked,

"Magic mirror on the wall,
Who is the fairest of us all?"

The mirror answered,

"Oh, Lady Queen, thou still art fair,
But none to Snow White can compare;
Deep within the forest glen,
She lives with seven little men."

The Queen was furious. She decided to kill Snow White herself. Taking off her palace gown, she dressed herself as a peddler woman. Then she set out for the forest with a basket of fruit on her arm. In the basket was a fine rosy apple, filled with magic poison.

When she came to the cottage, the wicked stepmother found Snow White at the window, darning a little sock.

"Good day, pretty maid," said the disguised stepmother. "I have some nice apples to sell." She held up the shiny red apple that was poisoned.

The Seven Dwarfs had warned Snow White not to let anybody in while they were away in the mountains. So she said, "I cannot let you in." But the apple looked so fresh and inviting that she reached out and took it. No sooner had she taken her first bite, than she fell on the floor in a dead faint.

The stepmother laughed as she hurried back through the woods. "Now I am the fairest in the land," she said to herself.

It was a sad sight that met the Dwarfs when they returned to the cottage. Their beloved Snow White was lying quiet and still on the floor. They wept and wept, but try as they might they could not bring her back to life.

Snow White looked so beautiful that the Dwarfs decided to place her in a glass case. Then they carried her to a hilltop, where they took turns keeping watch.

One day, a handsome Prince from a far country rode by. He looked at the lovely girl in the glass case, and fell in love with her. He begged the Dwarfs to let him take Snow White with him. "I cannot live without her," he pleaded. The Dwarfs gave their consent.

As the Prince lifted the case, the piece of poisoned apple fell out of Snow White's lips. She came to life again, and sat up.

"How did I get here? And who are you?" she said to the Prince. The Prince and the Dwarfs were overcome with joy. They told her all that had happened.

Then the Prince fell on his knees before Snow White. "Will you come with me and be my bride?" he asked. And so charming did he look that Snow White said, "Yes." Then Snow White thanked the Dwarfs for all that they had done for her, and rode off with the Prince.

A great wedding feast was proclaimed. The palace was decked with brilliant lights, velvet draperies and gorgeous flowers. Snow White's stepmother was among the people invited to the wedding, but she did not know that Snow White was to be the Prince's bride.

After dressing herself in her finest clothes, the stepmother Queen went to her mirror, and asked,

"Magic mirror on the wall,
Who is the fairest of us all?"

The mirror replied,

"Oh, Queen, thou hast a beauty rare,
But Snow White, the Prince's bride,
Is still more fair."

The Queen turned pale in amazement and rage. She struck at the magic mirror. And as the mirror fell to the floor in fragments, the wicked stepmother fell dead. Never again would she harm Snow White.

The wedding feast was very gay, and the dancing and festivities lasted all through the night and the next day. And Snow White and the Prince lived happily ever after.

Diamonds and Toads

THERE was once upon a time a widow who had two daughters. The eldest was so much like her in the face and disposition that whoever looked upon the daughter saw the mother. They were both so disagreeable and so proud that there was no living with them.

The youngest, who was the very picture of her father for courtesy and sweetness of temper, was one of the most beautiful girls ever seen. As people naturally love their own likeness, this mother doted on her eldest daughter, and at the same time had a horrible dislike for the youngest— she made her eat scraps from the kitchen and work continually.

Among other things, this poor child was forced twice a day to travel as far as a mile and a half away from the house to draw water and then to bring back a full pitcher. One day, when she was at the fountain, there came to her a poor woman, who begged her for a drink.

"Oh yes, with all my heart, ma'am," said this pretty little girl; and rinsing the pitcher immediately, she took up some water from the clearest part of the fountain, and gave it to the poor woman, holding up the pitcher all the while, that she might drink more easily.

The poor woman having drunk, said to her:

"You are so very pretty, my dear, so good and so mannerly, that I cannot help giving you a gift." For this was a fairy who had taken the form of a poor country woman to see just how kind and well-mannered this pretty girl could be. "I will give you a gift," continued the Fairy, "so that, at every word you speak, there shall come out of your mouth either a flower or a jewel."

When the girl came home her mother scolded her for staying so long at the fountain.

"I beg your pardon, Mamma," said the poor girl, "for not hurrying."

And in speaking these words there came out of her mouth two roses, two pearls, and two diamonds.

"What is it I see there?" said her mother, quite astonished. "I think I see pearls and diamonds come out of the girl's mouth! How did this happen, child?"

This was the first time she ever called her "child."

The poor creature told her the entire story of how this had come about and as she spoke an enormous number of diamonds came out of her mouth.

"In good faith," cried the mother, "what's good for one daughter is good for the other. Come here, girl; look what comes out of your sister's mouth when she speaks. Would you not be glad, my dear, for the same gift? You have nothing else to do but go and draw water out of the fountain, and when a certain poor woman asks you to let her drink, you must give it to her very politely."

"That will be the day," said this ill-bred sister, "when I go draw water."

"You shall go!" said the mother, "and this very minute!"

So away she went, but grumbling all the way, taking with her the best silver tankard in the house.

She was no sooner at the fountain than she saw coming out of the wood a lady most gloriously dressed, who came up to her, and asked to drink. This was, you must know, the very fairy who appeared to her sister, but had now taken the air and dress of a princess, to see just how rude and unmannerly this saucy girl could be.

"Am I here," said the proud, saucy girl, "to wait on the likes of you? Get your own water."

"You are not very kind," answered the Fairy, without putting herself in a great stir. "Well then, since you have so little breeding, and are so rude, I will give you a gift so that at every word you speak there shall come out of your mouth a snake or a toad."

So soon as her mother saw her coming she cried out:

"Well, daughter?"

"Well, mother?" answered the nasty girl, throwing out of her mouth two vipers and two toads.

"Oh! mercy," cried the mother; "what is it I see? Oh! it is that wretch your sister who brought this on us; but she shall pay for it;" and immediately she ran to beat her. The poor child fled away from her, and went to hide herself in the forest not far from there.

The King's son, on his return from hunting, met her, and seeing her so very pretty, asked her what she did there alone and why she wept.

"Alas! sir, my mamma has turned me out of doors."

The King's son, who saw five or six pearls and as many diamonds come out of her mouth, desired her to tell him how that happened. She thereupon told him the whole story; and so the King's son fell in love with her, and, considering that such a gift was worth more than any marriage dowry, took her to the palace of the King and that very day married her.

As for her sister, she made herself so hated that her own mother turned her out and the miserable wretch, having wandered about a good while without finding anybody to take her in, went to a corner of the wood, and died.

The Snow Queen

A Fairy Tale in Seven Stories

The First Story

Of the Mirror and Its Fragments

IT is best to always begin at the beginning. When we have got to the end of the story, we will know more than we do now, but in the meantime know that it was a Goblin who started it all, and he was one of the very worst.

One day, this Goblin was in the best of moods, for he had created a mirror. It wasn't an ordinary mirror by any means; everything it reflected seemed to shrink and shrivel and look the worst it possibly could. Beautiful landscapes appeared in it like so much boiled spinach; pretty people looked distorted and ugly, and if they had so much as a freckle, it spread over the whole of their faces.

The Goblin thought this was exceedingly funny, and when he showed it around to all his goblin friends they agreed that it was a marvellous invention.

"Now," they said among themselves, "the world will see what it really looks like." They carried the mirror far and wide, until there was not a person nor a place that had not been distorted in its terrible reflection. But that was not enough for the goblins; they wanted to fly to heaven with it, in order to make fun of the angels.

Higher and higher they flew with the mirror, until they came quite close to heaven itself. And then the mirror trembled and shook so that it jumped out of their hands and fell to the earth, shattering into a hundred million billion pieces and more. There it caused even more mischief than before, for some of the fragments were no larger than a grain of sand, and these flew around the wide world! And when these pieces got into the eyes of people, there they remained. These poor folk then saw everything in reverse, or only had eyes for the wrong side of things, for every tiny fragment of the mirror had the same quality as the whole.

There were pieces of it large enough to be used for windowpanes, but then it was not wise to look through them at one's neighbours, and smaller pieces of the glass were made into spectacles, but alas, they made the vision worse instead of better. And there were even some who got a little bit of it right in their hearts. And this was the worst thing of all; for then it turned the heart into a lump of ice.

The Goblin laughed and laughed at all the mischief he had caused until he almost split from it.

But the fragments of the mirror still floated around the world.

And now you shall hear something about them.

The Second Story

A Little Boy and a Little Girl

In a large city, where there are so many houses and people that there isn't room enough for everyone to have a little garden, and folks must be satisfied with plants in little flower pots, lived two poor children.

They were not brother and sister, but they loved one another just as though they were. They lived opposite each other high up in two attic rooms. Where the roof of one house joined that of the other, the children's parents had placed two large flower boxes, and they looked very pretty there, growing herbs for the kitchen, and sweet peas, and a rose tree for each.

In the summer, the children were allowed to sit and play by the flowers, singing songs and making up little games under the rose trees. In the winter though, this pleasure came to an end, and they would warm pennies on the stove to make peep holes in the ice that covered the windowpanes. The boy's name was Kay and the girl's name was Gerda.

Outside the snow whirled all around, covering everything in a blanket of white.

"It is the white bees that are swarming," the Grandmother told them.

"Have they also a Queen bee?" asked Kay, for he knew that all bees have their Queen.

"Oh yes," answered the Grandmother, "she flies about when the swarm is the thickest. She is the largest of them all; she never falls to earth, but floats back again into the black sky. On winter nights she flies about the town and peeps in at the windows, and freezes them up in a wonderful way, as though they were covered with flowers."

"We have seen that," cried both the children, and they knew her story must be true.

"But, can the Snow Queen come in here?" asked Gerda.

"Let her come," Kay answered her, "I will put her on the stove till she melts."

But the Grandmother stroked his hair, and told them other stories.

That night, when Kay was back in his own house and dressed for bed, he crept up to one of the chairs by the window and looked out into the world. A few snowflakes were falling outside, and one of them remained, lying on the edge of the flower box. The snowflake began to grow larger and larger, until at last it became a little lady, dressed in a fine white gown made of millions of little crystals. She was very beautiful and delicate, but all made of ice—dazzling, glittering, ice. And yet she was alive. Her eyes twinkled like shimmering stars, but there was no peace or rest in them. She nodded toward the window and beckoned to Kay with her hand. He grew frightened and jumped down from his chair by the window; and all at once the ice lady seemed to change to a great white bird that flew past his window with a beating of its wings. The next day there was a clear frost, and then it thawed at last.

The spring came again, the sun shone, and the children were allowed to sit once more in their little roof garden. The roses bloomed more beautifully than ever before. It seemed as though the summer would last forever. Kay and Gerda sat under the rose trees and looked at their picture books and sang songs to each other.

Then one evening, just as the clock was striking five—Kay jumped up with a cry of pain. "Oh! Something has struck me in the heart, and now I have something in my eye." Gerda flung her arms around Kay's neck to comfort him; he blinked his eyes, but there was nothing to be seen. "I think it has gone," he said, but it was not gone at all. It was one of the fragments from the Goblin's terrible mirror. And poor little Kay was caught with pieces of it in his eye and in his heart. The fragments no longer hurt him—but they were still there. He turned to his friend.

"What are you crying for? It makes you look all ugly and wrinkled up. And look at the roses! Why they're all worm–eaten and crooked." He kicked the flower box with his foot, and started tearing at the roses with his hands.

"Kay, what are you doing?" cried the little girl. "What is the matter with you?" But when he saw how frightened she was, he only laughed and started tearing at the roses again, and then ran off down the stairs.

After that, he changed completely. Whenever Grandmother told stories, he laughed and interrupted her, and hid her glasses whenever he could. He would go behind people's backs and imitate them, and everyone got to thinking he was very clever, for he could make fun of nearly everyone. But it was all due to the fragment of mirror in his heart, and that which was in his eye. He even teased little Gerda, who loved him better than anyone in the world. Even his games were different than they had been. One winter's day, when the snowflakes were whirling about, he took a large magnifying glass from his pocket, and called Gerda to his side.

"You see?" he said. "Snowflakes are so much better than real flowers; each one is different, but each is perfect. If only they would not melt!"

Soon after that, he ran off without her, and went to go sledding with the older boys in the square. There, the boys would often fasten their sleds to the sleighs of the people going by, and ride with them all around the town.

Just as he was playing there, Kay saw a large, white sleigh come by. Inside sat someone wrapped from head to toes in white fur. The sleigh went twice round the square; Kay quickly tied his sled to the back of it, and off they went. The driver turned around and nodded to Kay in quite a friendly manner, as though they knew one another. But though he thought hard about who it could be, he could not see who it was, all wrapped in fur. They rode on for quite a distance. Whenever Kay thought of untying his sled, the driver would nod again to him, and he stayed where he was. They drove out through the gates of the town, and the snow began to fall so thickly that Kay could hardly see where he was.

He grew frightened and tried to untie the sled, but it was bound fast. Off they went into the swiftness of the wind. He cried aloud, but there was no one to hear him. The sleigh flew on. The snowflakes grew larger and larger, until it seemed to Kay as though he were surrounded by a flock of white birds. Then, all at once they flew aside, and the big sleigh stopped. The driver stood up and Kay saw that the fur was made of the purest snow. It was a lady—tall and slender and dazzling white—it was the Snow Queen!

"We have driven well," she told him, "but why do you shiver so? Creep into my fur." She seated him in the sleigh beside her, and it seemed to Kay as though he'd sunk in a snowdrift. "Are you still shivering?" she asked, and kissed him on the forehead. Ugh! Her kiss was colder than ice; it went straight into his heart, and he felt as though he were about to die. But it was only for a moment, for she kissed him again, and he forgot little Gerda, and his Grandmother, and all at home.

"Now you must not have another kiss," the Snow Queen told him, "or I might kiss you to death!"

Kay looked at her—she was very beautiful. She did not seem to be made of ice, as she had when she had beckoned to him from the window. In his eyes she was perfect, and he was not at all afraid. He began to tell her all the things he knew; about the multiplication tables, and how many people lived in his town, and all the rest he could think of. But she only smiled at him, and he began to understand that perhaps he did not know very much at all.

Then it seemed to him as though they flew together up into the black sky, while the storm whistled and howled all around them, as though it were singing ancient songs. They flew over forests and lakes and land and sea. Beneath them the cold wind whistled; the wolves howled; and over the glistening snow flew black, screaming crows. But beyond the moon shone large and bright in the sky, and Kay gazed after it through the long, long, winter's night. And by day he slept at the feet of the Snow Queen.

The Third Story

The Flower Garden of The Woman Who Knew Magic

But how did Gerda get on when Kay did not return? No one knew what had become of him; nobody knew where he was. There were those who believed he had drowned in the river that flowed through the town, and when Gerda heard that, she wept long and bitterly.

At last the spring came once again, and the sun shone warm.

"Kay is dead and gone!" said little Gerda.

"I do not believe that," said the sunshine.

"He is dead and gone!" she told the birds.

"We do not believe that," they replied.

Gerda thought hard about it. "I will put on my new red shoes," she told herself, "the shoes that Kay has never seen, and I will go down and beg the river to give him back." Then, early the next morning, she kissed her mother, who was still asleep, put on her new red shoes, and went out of the town gate down to the river bank.

"Is it true you have taken Kay?" she asked the waters. "I will give you my new red shoes if you will give him back to me."

It seemed to her as though the waves were nodding to her. She took off her shoes and threw them into the water, but they fell close to shore, and the little waves carried them right back to the bank. The river did not want to accept her treasure because it had not taken little Kay at all; but Gerda only thought it was because she had not thrown them far enough out into the water. So she crept into a little boat that was tied on the bank and threw the shoes off the far end.

But the boat was not tied securely, and her movement caused it to drift from the shore and out into the water. She tried to get out, but was now so far away she could not get back to the shore, and the boat drifted farther and farther downstream.

Gerda grew very afraid, and began to cry. Hour after hour she drifted down the river, until at last she began to think that the river might be carrying her to Kay, so she sat up and began to look around her. Then she came to a great cherry orchard, in the middle of which stood a little house.

It was a pretty place, with red and blue windows, and a thatched roof. Outside stood two wooden soldiers. Gerda called out to them, but of course, they gave no answer. The river carried the boat right up to the bank, and Gerda called out louder, and an old woman came out of the house, leaning on a crutch.

"Poor child," the woman said, "what brings you out here on the broad river, floating so far out into the world?"

And the old woman went straight out into the water, seized the boat with the end of her crutch and pulled Gerda to shore. She lifted her out of the boat, and Gerda was only too glad to be on dry land once again.

"Come and tell me who you are, and how you came here," said the old lady. And Gerda told her everything there was to tell. The old woman shook her head and said, "Hmm, hmmm." When Gerda got finished with the story, she then asked her if she had seen little Kay. The old lady told her that she had not seen him, but that he would most likely pass this way if she cared to wait. Meanwhile, she said, Gerda shouldn't be worried for him; she might taste the cherries, and play in her garden. The old woman said that her flowers were better than any in the world, for each of them could tell a story of its own.

She took Gerda by the hand, led her into the little house, and locked the door.

Inside, it was very beautiful, for the sun came in through the coloured windowpanes in various colours—like a prism. On the table were some very fine cherries, and Gerda ate them to her heart's content. While she ate, the woman combed her hair with a golden comb, until her curls shone round her face.

"I have long wished for a little girl like you," said the old woman. "How nicely we will get along." And as she combed her hair, Gerda began to forget all about Kay, for the old lady knew magic, though she was not a wicked witch. She only cast a few little spells for her own pleasure, and she was very anxious to keep little Gerda.

Then the old woman went out into the garden, and pointed her crutch at all the rose trees until they sank into the earth. She did not want Gerda to be reminded of why she had come.

After the roses had disappeared, she took Gerda out into the flower garden, where the little girl was so happy she jumped for joy. Every flower she had ever heard of was there blooming in every colour she knew. She played there until the sun went down, and the old woman put her to bed on red silk pillows stuffed with violets.

When morning came, she was again allowed to play in the garden, and so it was that many days went by. And though it seemed to Gerda as though something were missing from that beautiful place, she was never sure what it was until one day she sat gazing at the old lady's hat, and saw a rose on the brim.

The old lady had forgotten to remove it when she made the other roses disappear, which is exactly the kind of thing that happens when you don't keep your wits about you.

"Why!" said Gerda, "There are no roses here." And she ran in and out of the flower beds, searching for the roses, but there were none to be found.

She sat down and wept, thinking of all the time she had wasted in the garden. Her tears fell upon a spot where a rose tree was buried, and all at once it rose up out of the ground, full of blossoms. Gerda kissed it and thought of the beautiful roses at home, and of little Kay.

"I came to find Kay," she told the rose tree. "Do you know where he is? Do you believe he is dead and gone?"

"He is not dead," said the Roses. "We have been under the ground, where the dead people are, and he is not there."

"Oh, thank you," said Gerda and went looking round at all the other flowers, asking if they had seen Kay.

But each flower stood in the sun dreaming her own dreams. They told Gerda many stories, but none were about Kay.

And what did the Tiger-lily say?

"Do you hear the drum? Booom-booom. It knows only two notes: boom! boom! Listen to the wailing of the women! The Hindu woman stands on the pyre, dressed in a long red robe, and the flames surround her and her dead husband. But the woman dreams of the living man, whose eyes burn with a fiercer fire than that which consumes her. Must the flames of the heart die in the funeral fire?"

"I do not understand you," said Gerda.

"That is my story." said the lily.

What said the Convolvulus?

"Overhanging the highway stands an ancient castle, covered with ivy. It climbs over the red walls, leaf over leaf, to the balcony where a lady stands. She bends over the railings and looks to the road. No rose hangs fresher from its branch than she—no apple blossom floats more lightly on the wind. Listen to the rustle of her silken robes. 'Will he never come?' she asks."

"Do you mean Kay?" asked Gerda.

"I can only tell my tale," said the Convolvulus. "I only know my dream."

And what did the Snowdrop say?

"Between the trees hangs a swing. Two pretty girls in white frocks and fluttering green ribbons sit and swing. Their brother stands behind them, and winds his arm around the rope swing to steady himself. He is blowing soap bubbles from a little pipe. The swing moves to and fro, the bubbles swing out over the yard. The swing moves to and fro; a little dog jumps up and tries to play. The swing knocks him down and he barks at the children, angry at their games. The bubbles burst. A wooden swing—a fluttering picture. That is all I have to tell."

"What you have to tell me is very pretty, but you speak sadly, and do not mention Kay at all," said Gerda.

What said the Hyacinth?

"There were three beautiful sisters, each transparent and delicate. One wore a gown of red, one of blue, and one of white. Hand in hand they danced in the moonlight by the shore of a lake. They were not fairies, but human children. There was a sweet fragrance in the air, and they went to the forest to search it out. The fragrance grew stronger. Three coffins, in which lay the beautiful maidens, glided from the forest to the lake; fire-flies shone like floating candles. Do the dancing maidens sleep—or are they dead? The flower scent says they have ceased to live. The bells are tolling their farewell."

"You make me sad," said Gerda. "Your perfume is so strong I cannot help but weep for those maidens. Oh! Is Kay really dead? The roses have been under the earth, and they say no."

"Our bells toll not for Kay," rang the Hyacinths, "we know him not. We sing our own song, the only one we know."

And Gerda went to the Buttercup, which was gleaming through the fresh green leaves. "You are a bright little sun!" said Gerda. "Tell me if you know where I can find him."

The Buttercup shone brightly, gazing at little Gerda. What could it sing? But its song was not about Kay—

"The sun was shining cheerfully on the first day of spring. Its rays streamed over the neighbour's wall, and close by the yellow flowers bloomed—sparkling like gold in the light. Old Grandmother was out in her chair; her granddaughter, a pretty servant-maid, came to her and kissed her. There was gold, too, in the kiss, gold in the heart—gold in the early morning hour. That is my little story," said the Buttercup.

Oh, thought Gerda, how Grandmother must miss me! She must be as sorry for me as she was for Kay! But I will soon come back, and I'll bring Kay with me, too. But it isn't any use at all to ask the flowers. They only know their own songs; they can give me no good advice.

And then she began to run to the edge of the garden, but the Narcissus struck her on the leg as she passed. She stopped, looking at the tall flower, and asked: "Do you, perhaps, know anything?" And what did it say?

"I can see myself! I can see myself!" said the Narcissus. "What a beautiful perfume I have! High up in a window stands a half-dressed ballerina. She stands on one leg, now on both, and kicks at all the world. But she is only an illusion. She is pouring water from a teapot over a piece of cloth she is holding. It is her blouse. On a peg hangs a linen skirt which has also been washed in the teapot and dried on the roof. She puts it on, and ties a yellow scarf around her neck—and the dress looks whiter than before. One leg in the air!—see how straight she stands on one stalk! I can see myself! I can see myself!"

"I don't care a bit about that!" Gerda said. "That is nothing to do with me!" And so she ran to the far end of the garden. The gate was locked, but she pulled at the rusty hinges until it gave way; the door sprang open and Gerda ran out barefooted into the wide world. She looked behind her three times, but there was no one following her, and then at last she stopped to rest.

She sat down on a stone and looked around her. The summer was gone. It was late in the autumn, but she had not seen it in the old woman's garden. There had always been sunshine there, and the flowers bloomed regardless of the season.

"Oh, dear," she said aloud. "How I have wasted my time! It is already autumn and I must not rest." And she rose up to go.

Her feet were sore and weary. Everything around her was cold and rough; the long willow leaves were gone yellow and the mist fell from them like water—and all around her the leaves were falling. Only the sloe-tree still bore fruit; and it was so sour it set the teeth on edge.

It seemed all grey and gloomy out in the wide world.

The Fourth Story

The Prince and the Princess

At last Gerda had to rest again. All at once a big crow came hopping towards her, and stopped just opposite to where she sat. He sat a long while looking at her; turning his head from side to side; "Caw!" he said, "Good day, good day!" He could not speak very plainly, but meant to be kind to Gerda, and he asked her what she was doing all by herself out in the world.

Gerda told him the whole of her story and all of her adventures, and asked the Crow if he had seen Kay.

The Crow nodded very gravely and said: "That may be! That may be!"

"What? Do you really think so?" Gerda nearly squeezed the Crow to death so heartily did she kiss him.

"Gently, gently," said the Crow. "It might be him—but by this time he has probably forgotten you for the Princess."

"Does he live with a Princess?" Gerda was astounded.

"Yes, listen," said the Crow. "But it is very difficult for me to speak your language. If you knew the crow language, I could tell you much better."

"No, I never learned that," Gerda answered. "Grandmother knew it though, and some others too."

"It doesn't matter," said the Crow, "I will tell you the story as well as I can, but it will be bad at the best."

And so he told what he knew—

"In the kingdom where we are now, lives a very, very, smart Princess. She has read all the newspapers in the whole world and forgotten them again, so learned is she. One day, as she was sitting on her throne, (and that is not all it's made out to be, they say,) she sang herself a little song that went:

'Why should I not married be?'

'There's something in that!' she said to herself, and so she decided to get married. But first, she had to find herself a husband. And not just anyone would do. She wanted one that would speak when he was spoken to, and not just sit about looking handsome, for that is so tiresome. And so she summoned all her maids of honour, who thought it was a wonderful idea—

"You may be sure," the Crow continued, "that all I am telling you is true, for I have a tame sweetheart who hops about the palace all day long and has told me everything." She was of course, a crow also—for it is just as they say! Birds of a feather flock together.

"The next day, the newspapers announced that anyone who was young and good-looking might come and talk with the Princess, who would choose for her husband the one whose conversation showed he was the most at ease.

"It's as true as I'm sitting here," said the Crow. "People from all around came flocking in. There was a good deal of crowding and pushing, but no one succeeded on the first or the second day.

"It seems they could speak well enough when they were out in the street, but once they were in the presence of the Princess they got quite confused, and had nothing whatever to say.

"All they could do was to say over again the last word the Princess had said, which of course, she had no particular interest in hearing over again.

"Anyway, the procession continued for a while, all the way from the town gate to the palace. I myself went to see it," said the Crow.

"But Kay," said Gerda, "what about Kay? Did you see him?"

"Wait a minute, I was just coming to him. It was on the third day there came a little fellow, without horse or carriage, right up to the palace gates. His eyes sparkled just like yours do, and he had beautiful long hair. But his clothes were very poor."

"That was Kay! That was Kay!" Gerda clapped her hands in great delight. "Oh, then I have found him at last!"

"He had a little knapsack on his back," said the Crow.

"No, I'm sure it wasn't;" Gerda answered him, "it might have been his sled. He went away with a sled."

"That might be true, I did not take much notice," said the Crow. "But this much I do know from my sweetheart. When he got through the gates and into the palace, and passed the guards and lackeys all dressed in gold and silver, he was not in the least confused. He only nodded and said to them—'It must be tiresome to spend the day standing around on the stairs, I'd rather go in.' The halls were glittering with light, Privy Councillors and Excellencies of all sorts were walking around in bare feet, carrying golden vessels. It was enough to make one feel serious. I heard that his boots creaked in the worst way, but he was not in the least bit shy, and went right before the Princess."

"I know that it was Kay!" said Gerda. "His boots creaked like that, I heard them!"

"Well," said the Crow, "they did creak. But he went boldly up to the Princess herself, who was sitting on a pearl as big as a spinning wheel. And there were all the maids of honour and courtiers, who in turn had all their own servants standing about, and the nearer they were to the door, the prouder they looked."

"That must have been terrible!" said Gerda. "And he still won the Princess?"

"If I had not been a crow I would have married her myself, although I am engaged. They say he spoke as well as I do when I speak the crow language. He was most merry and handsome, and said that he had not come to woo the Princess, but only to find out how wise she was. All in all, he was pleased with her, and she with him."

"Of course that was Kay!" cried Gerda. "He was so clever he knew the multiplication tables. Oh, will you not lead me to the castle too?"

"That is easy to say," said the Crow, "but how are we to manage it? I will go to the palace and talk it over with my sweetheart; she may be able to help. But I must tell you—a little girl like you will never get permission to go right in."

"Yes, I shall," said Gerda, "once Kay hears that I am there, he will come down himself and bring me in."

"Wait for me over by that gate," said the Crow. And he wagged his head and flew away.

Late in the evening, after it was dark, he returned.

"Caw! Caw!" he said. "My sweetheart sends you greetings, and here is a little loaf of bread for you. She took it from the kitchen. They have plenty, and you must be hungry. But it is impossible for you to get into the palace. You are barefoot, and all the guards and golden lackeys will never allow it. But don't cry, we shall get in all the same. My sweetheart knows a little back staircase that leads to their bedroom, and she knows too, where she can get the key."

The Crow led Gerda to the grand avenue leading to the palace, and oh, how her heart beat within her! It seemed as though she were about to do something she shouldn't, yet it was only that she wanted to know if it was Kay. It must be! How well she remembered his eyes and his hair. And she had come so far to see him, and hoped he would be glad to see her at last.

Now, they were on the staircase. A little lamp was burning, and Gerda could see the tame Crow waiting for them, turning her head from side to side and looking at Gerda. Gerda bowed as her Grandmother had taught her to do, and thanked the tame Crow for all her help.

"My beloved has spoken well of you, my little lady. Your life is very touching. Will you take the lamp, and I will lead the way? We must go right on, for I don't want to meet anyone."

"It almost seems as though there were someone behind us," said Gerda.

"Those are only the Dreams," said the Crow, "they come to take the thoughts of their Highnesses out hunting. It is just as well, for then you will be able to get a good look at them while they sleep. But remember, if you rise to honour and favour, be sure to show a grateful heart."

They went from one great hall to another, each more splendid and beautiful than the last. It was enough to bewilder one. Then, all at once it seemed they were in the bedchamber of the Prince and Princess. The ceiling looked like a great palm tree hung with leaves of crystal glass; and in the middle of the floor hung two beds from a single stalk of gold. The beds looked like lilies swaying back and forth—one red, one white. In the white bed lay the Princess and in the red—there Gerda expected to find Kay. She drew one of the curtains aside and saw a sweet little brown neck. Oh! It must be Kay! She called his name aloud and held the lamp closer to his head. The Dreams came rushing in—all on horseback; he awoke, turned his head and—it was not him!

The Prince was only like him in the neck, but nevertheless he was young and handsome. The Princess looked out from the white lily, and asked who was there. Gerda began to weep as though her heart would break, and told them the whole story, and all that the Crows had done for her.

They praised the Crows, and assured them they would be rewarded. The Prince arose and offered Gerda his bed for the night; more than that he could not do.

She lay down, folded her hands, and was fast asleep. All the Dreams came flying in, looking like angels, and they drew a little sleigh. Kay sat upon it, nodding to her—but it was only a dream, and vanished when she woke again.

The next day she was dressed from head to foot in beautiful satin and velvet. The Prince and Princess invited her to stay with them and enjoy herself. But she only begged for a little carriage and a horse, and a little pair of boots; then she would go again into the world to find Kay.

And they not only gave her the boots, but a fur muff as well—and when she was ready to leave, a new coach of the purest gold drew up before the door. They helped her to the carriage themselves, and wished her all good fortune. Crow sat by Gerda's side for a time. Inside the coach, there were wonderful things for her to eat; it was lined with sugarplums and sweets, and there were ginger biscuits and fruits in the seat.

"Farewell! Farewell!" the Prince and Princess wept at her leaving. Gerda wept too, and so did the Crow. They went on for three miles together, until at last he too, had to say goodbye. He flew up to a tree, and beat his wings for as long as he could see the carriage riding down the road, glittering like the rays of the sun.

The Fifth Story

The Little Robber-Girl

They drove through the dark forest, but the golden coach gleamed like a torch, dazzling some robbers' eyes.

"It is gold! It is gold!" They ran forth and killed the coachmen, and then dragged Gerda from the carriage.

"She is fat!" they said. "She is pretty," said the old robber woman, who had a long beard, and eyebrows that hung down into her eyes. "She is as good as a lamb. How good she will taste!" And with that, she drew a long knife from her belt that glittered horribly in the light.

"Oh!" she screamed at the same moment, for her own daughter had come up on her back and was biting her on the ear. "You wicked child!" And was prevented from killing little Gerda.

"She shall play with me," said the robber-girl. "She shall give me her muff and her pretty dress and sleep with me in my bed." And with that she bit her mother again.

"I want to get into the carriage," said the robber-girl, and started to climb right up, because she was so spoilt and stubborn. She and Gerda sat and drove deep into the forest. The girl was almost as big as Gerda, but much stronger, with broad shoulders and sad, dark eyes. She clasped Gerda around the waist and whispered: "They shall not kill you as long as I do not get angry with you. You are surely a Princess."

"No," Gerda told her, "I am not—" and then she told the girl all that had happened, and how she was searching for Kay.

The girl looked at Gerda quite seriously, dried her eyes and said: "They shall not kill you even if I do get angry with you. I will do it myself."

At last the coach stopped before the robber's castle, an old horrible place whose walls were cracked from top to bottom. They all went inside, where the fires burned, and meat roasted on the spits in a great old smoky hall.

"You shall sleep here with me tonight, and all my little pets" said the robber-girl.

They had something to eat and drink, and then went to a corner where some straw mats were spread. All around, a hundred pigeons sat, perched on the beams above them. They appeared to be asleep, but they rustled and coo'ed among themselves when the two girls approached.

"They are all mine," said the robber-girl, and she seized one of the nearest and shook it until it flapped its wings in Gerda's face. "Kiss it!" she cried. "Those are the wood pigeons over there," and she pointed to the rafter above them. "And this is my old sweetheart, Ba!" she said as she pulled a reindeer out by its horn. It had a polished copper ring around its neck, and was tied up.

"I have to keep him well tied," the robber-girl said, "or he would run away from me. Every evening I tickle him with my knife; he's so afraid of that."

And with that she drew a long knife from a hole in the wall and drew it lightly over the reindeer's neck. The poor creature kicked and the girl laughed aloud, and drew Gerda into bed with her.

"Do you keep the knife with you while you sleep?" asked Gerda.

"I always sleep with a knife," the robber-girl replied, "you never know what will happen. But tell me again about Kay, and why you came out into the wide world."

So Gerda told her again from the beginning; the pigeons cooed up in their cages, and all slept. But Gerda could not close her eyes at all—she did not know whether she was to live or to die.

Then the wood pigeons began to coo to her, "We have seen him! We have seen little Kay. A white hen was pulling his sled. He sat in the Snow Queen's sleigh and they flew high up over the forest when we were lying in our nests. She blew on us little ones and all died, save for us two. Coo! Coo!"

"What are you saying?" cried Gerda. "Which way was the Snow Queen travelling? Do you know anything about it?"

"She was probably going to Lapland," said the pigeons, "for they have snow and ice there always. Ask the reindeer."

"There is ice and snow there," said the Reindeer. "It is a beautiful place. There the Snow Queen has her summer castle—her real home is up at the North Pole."

"Oh Kay,—" sighed Gerda.

"Lie still, or I will put my knife in you," said the robber-girl.

In the morning, Gerda told her all the pigeons had said, and the robber-girl looked at her quite seriously and said: "It's all the same, it's all the same! Do you know where Lapland is?" she asked the Reindeer.

"Who should know better than I?" said the Reindeer. "I was born and bred there, I ran about in the snow fields." And his eyes sparkled.

"Listen!" said the robber-girl. "Wait until all the men have gone away. Only my mother is here and she will stay, but later in the morning she will drink from the big bottle and sleep for a time. Then I will do something for you."

Later, when the mother had drunk and was fast asleep the robber-girl went to the Reindeer and said, "I should like to keep you, and tickle you with my knife, for you are so funny then. But never mind, I will loosen your rope and help you out, so that you might run to Lapland; but you must make good use of your legs, and carry this little girl to where the Snow Queen lives."

The Reindeer sprang up with happiness. The robber-girl lifted Gerda up on its back, and took care to see that she was secure, and even gave her a little cushion to sit on.

"Here are your fur boots," she said, "for it will be cold; but I will keep your muff, for it is too pretty to give up. But you will not be cold, for here are my mother's big mittens—they reach almost to your elbows. Put them on; there now, your hands look just like my ugly old mother's."

And Gerda wept for joy.

"I can't bear to see you cry—now, you must be happy. And here are two loaves of bread for you and a ham, so that you won't be hungry." And with that, she opened the door, cut the Reindeer's rope with her long knife and said:

"Now run! But take good care of the little girl!"

And the Reindeer ran. They crossed over fields and marshes and rock and stone until it seemed as though the sky were on fire, sneezing red flames.

"Those are my old Northern Lights," said the Reindeer—"see how they glow!" And they ran on, faster than ever, day and night. The bread was eaten, then the ham and then they found themselves in Lapland.

The Sixth Story

The Lapp Woman and the Finn Woman

They stopped at a little hut. It was very poor-looking, and its roof sloped almost to the ground. The door was so low that anyone who wanted to go in or out had to crawl about on their hands and knees.

There was no one at home but an old Lapp woman who was frying fish by the light of a lamp. The Reindeer told her all Gerda's history; but first told his own; for it seemed to him that it was the more important. Gerda was so cold and exhausted from her travels that she could not speak.

"You poor things!" said the Lapp woman. "You have yet a long way to go. It is more than a hundred miles to Finland, for the Snow Queen is staying there in the country burning Bengal lights every evening. I will write a few words for you and you can take them to the Finn woman, for she can give you better information than I."

When Gerda had warmed herself and had something to eat, the Lapp woman took a piece of dry codfish, for she had no paper, and wrote a note to the Finn woman. She told Gerda to take care of it, tied her to the Reindeer's back, and they ran on again. The Northern Lights glowed through the night and lighted their way all the way to Finland.

They knocked at the chimney of the Finland woman, for she didn't even have a door. It was so hot inside that she went about the house almost naked. She was very small and always grumbling to herself about one thing and another. She loosened Gerda's mittens and boots, and laid some ice on the Reindeer's head, for otherwise it would have been too hot for them. Then she read what was written on the codfish. Three times she read it through, until she knew it by heart, and then popped the fish into the saucepan, for it was good to eat, and she never wasted anything.

Then the Reindeer told his story, and then Gerda's after that. The Finn woman blinked her clever eyes, but said nothing until he was done.

"You are so clever," said the Reindeer. "I know you can tie all the winds of the world together with a little bit of string. If a sailor unties one knot, he has a good wind, if he loosens the second, it blows hard; but if he unties the third and the fourth, there comes a storm fierce enough to uproot all the trees in the forest. Can you give Gerda something to drink so that she will have the power of twelve men—and can overcome the Snow Queen?"

"Twelve men's power!" said the Finn woman. "Much use that would be!" Then she went to a shelf and took down an old parchment covered with mysterious writings. She read until the perspiration streamed from her forehead.

But the Reindeer begged again for Gerda, and looked so earnestly at the Finn woman that she began to blink again. Then she drew the Reindeer into a corner and whispered: "Little Kay is certainly at the Snow Queen's—and happy to be there, too. He thinks it is the best place in the world; but that is because he has a splinter of glass in his eye and in his heart. These must be got out, or he will never be human again. The Snow Queen will hold him in her power forever."

"But can you not give little Gerda something that will give her power over them all?"

"I can give her no greater power than she has already. Don't you see how great that is? Don't you see how man and beast have got to serve her? How else would she have come so far in her bare feet? If she can't reach the Snow Queen by herself, then we cannot help her. Her power is in her heart—she must come to know it by herself. Carry the girl to the Snow Queen's garden, and set her down by the bush that stands with its red berries in the snow. Then run back to me as fast as you can."

And then the Finn woman lifted Gerda onto the Reindeer's back, which ran as fast as it could.

"Oh, I haven't got boots—I haven't got mittens!" cried Gerda. She soon felt the lack of them in the terrible wind, but the Reindeer dared not stop, and they ran on, faster than ever. They came to the bush with the red berries, and there he set her down, kissed her on the mouth, and bright tears rolled down his neck.

Then he ran back as fast as he could, leaving her there in the ice and snow without boots nor mittens.

She ran forward as fast as she could. There came a whole regiment of snowflakes but they had not fallen from the sky—they ran along behind her and the nearer they came, the larger they seemed. Gerda remembered how the snowflakes had looked under the magnifying glass, but these were different—they were alive. Some were shaped like enormous porcupines; others formed like great knots of snakes stretching forth their heads.

Gerda tried to say her prayers, but the cold was so great that her breath poured out of her like smoke. The smoke formed itself into little transparent spirits, who grew larger as they touched the earth—armed with helmets and spears. They attacked the terrible snow sentries and Gerda went on bravely into the awful cold. The spirits stroked her hands and feet, and she felt the cold less than before, and hurried to the gates of the Snow Queen's palace.

In the meantime, we should see how little Kay was getting on. He was certainly not thinking of little Gerda, and least of all that she was standing at the palace gates.

The Seventh Story

What Happened in the Snow Queen's Palace and Afterwards

The walls of the palace were formed of the drifting snow—the doors and windows from the biting winds. There were more than a hundred halls, and the largest of them stretched for miles. They were lighted by the strongest of Northern Lights, and were frozen and empty— glittering in their iciness. There was never any laughter in those halls, nor any entertainments. The polar bears might have danced on their hind legs at a little ball, or the white foxes might have gossiped over tea in one of the halls, but it never came to pass.

Immense, vast and cold was the palace of the Snow Queen. In the midst of its never-ending halls was a great lake, frozen and broken up over its surface into thousands of bits, each exactly like the last, so that the pieces formed a perfect work of art. The Snow Queen sat in the very centre of it when she was at home. Then she said it was The Mirror of Reason, and that it was the best one in the world.

Little Kay was blue—no, almost black with the cold. But he never noticed it, for the Snow Queen had kissed away his shiverings, and his heart beat like a lump of ice inside him. He went about dragging some flat pieces of ice, joining them together like pieces of a puzzle. It was as if he wished to make something of them, taking the patterns apart and putting them together in different ways. He was playing the Game of Reason. In his eyes the patterns were the most beautiful things he knew, and the most important; but that was due to the grain of glass that was sticking into his eye. Time and again, he laid the pieces out to form a word—but he could never find the word he wanted—the word Eternity. And the Snow Queen had told him—"If you can find that figure—then you shall be your own master, and I will give you the whole world and a new pair of skates." But he could not.

"I must go away to warmer lands," said the Snow Queen. "I want to go and peep into the black cauldrons of Etna and Vesuvius, and I will whiten them a little. It does them good. And the grapes and the lemons, too." And away she flew.

Kay sat alone in the vast icy hall and looked at the pieces of ice. He thought and thought until something gave way inside him. He sat so still and frozen that one might have thought he was dead, after all.

At that moment Gerda stepped through the great gate and into the palace. The winds howled within, but she whispered to them, and they were silent, as if lulled to sleep. And she went on through the vast halls. She saw Kay sitting there, and knew him all at once. She threw her arms about his neck, crying, "Kay! Oh, Kay, I have found you at last!"

But he sat motionless, stiff and cold. Gerda began to cry and her tears fell upon his breast and thawed the lump of ice, melting even the little piece of the Goblin's mirror within it. He looked at her then and burst into tears himself, weeping so much that that splinter of glass washed out of his eye. He knew her then and cried out for joy, "Gerda, oh Gerda! Where have you been for so long a time? And where have I been?" He looked around him and said, "Oh, it is so terribly cold here. So large and empty!"

He clung to Gerda and they both laughed and wept for joy. It was so beautiful that even the pieces of ice got up and danced, and when they were still again they fell into letters that formed 'Eternity,' —the very word the Snow Queen had told him he must find if he were to be free, and have the whole world and a new pair of skates.

Gerda kissed his cheeks and they grew rosy, she kissed his eyes and they shone as bright as her own, she stroked his hands and feet, and he was healthy and cheerful once again. The Snow Queen might come home whenever she wished—his letters of freedom were there—formed in the ice. And they took each other by the hand and went from the palace. They talked of Grandmother, and the roses on the roof, and wherever they went the winds quieted, and the sun shone forth.

When they reached the bush with the red berries, the Reindeer was standing there waiting for them; it brought another reindeer with him whose udders were full, and they drank her warm milk and she kissed them.

They carried the two children first to the Finn woman who warmed them in her hut, and gave them directions for the journey home, and then to the Lapp woman, who made them new clothes and a sleigh to ride in. The Reindeer and his companion saw them to the borders of the country. There the green leaves were sprouting, and they all took leave of each other. The first birds of spring began to twitter and all the trees of the forest were in bud.

All at once a young girl came out of the wood riding a beautiful horse. Gerda knew them at once, for the horse was that which had drawn her golden coach. The girl had a little red cap on her head and a pair of pistols in her belt. It was the little robber-girl, who had grown tired of staying at home and was travelling north, and then, if that did not satisfy her, on to some other region.

She knew Gerda at once and it was a joyful meeting. "You're a fine one to go gadding," she told Kay. "I wonder whether you deserve to have someone running to the end of the world for your sake." Gerda patted her fondly on the cheek, and asked after the Prince and Princess.

"They are travelling in other countries," the robber-girl told them.

"But the Crow?" asked Gerda.

"The Crow is dead," she replied, "His tame sweetheart is now a widow and goes about pitying herself bitterly. But it is all nonsense. But tell me how you found each other."

And so Gerda and Kay both told their own story.

"So it's all right, then!" exclaimed the little robber-girl. And she took them both by the hand and wished them both well, promising that should she ever come through their town she would not fail to pay them a visit. Then she rode off into the wide world to see what she could find.

Gerda and Kay went hand in hand, and as they travelled the buds burst forth, and the birds sang, and all the world was clad in green. Church bells pealed out over the land and they recognized the steeples and towers of their own city. They went straight to Grandmother's door, up the stairs and into the room. Everything was in its usual place. The clock still said, tick-tock, tick-tock, but as Kay and Gerda passed through the room they noticed suddenly that they had grown up.

The roses on the roof bloomed by the open window, and they stood by their children's chairs holding each other by the hand. They had forgotten the splendour of the cold snow palace—it all seemed like some dream. Grandmother was sitting in her chair reading from the Bible.

"Unless ye be as little children, ye shall not enter the kingdom."

And Kay and Gerda looked into each other's eyes and understood. And so they sat for a time, grown up, and yet children.

And once again it was summer—warm, beautiful summer.

The Three Sillies

ONCE upon a time, when folks were not so wise as they are nowadays, there lived a farmer and his wife who had only one daughter. And she, being a pretty lass, was courted by a young squire.

Every evening he would stroll over from his castle to see her and stop to dine at the farm house, and every evening she would go down to the cellar to draw some cider for supper.

One evening, when she had gone down to draw the cider and had turned the tap as usual, she happened to look up at the ceiling, and there she saw a big wooden mallet stuck up in one of the beams.

It must have been there for ages and ages, for it was all covered with cobwebs; but somehow or another she had never noticed it before, and she got to thinking how dangerous it was to have the mallet there.

"Hmmm," thought she, "Supposing the young squire and me was to get married, and supposing we was to have a child, and supposing he came down to the cellar to draw cider like I'm doing, and supposing the mallet was to fall on his head and kill him! How dreadful that would be!"

And with that, she sat down and began to cry. And she cried and cried and cried.

Now, upstairs they began to wonder what was taking her so long; so, after awhile her mother came down to see what had become of her. She found the poor girl sitting on a cask, crying and crying, with cider running all over the floor.

"Good heavens!" cried her mother. "What ever is the matter?"

"Oh, mother," the girl said between her sobs, "it's that horrid mallet. Supposing the squire and me was married, and supposing we was to have a child, and supposing the little thing came down here to draw the cider like I'm doing, and supposing the mallet was to fall on his head and kill him. How dreadful that would be!"

"Oh my," said her mother, "that would be awful!" And she sat down beside her daughter and started to cry. And they both just sat and cried and cried. Now, when they did not come back, the farmer began to wonder what had happened, and went down to the cellar to find out. He found them both, sitting side by side, crying their eyes out, with cider running all over the floor.

"Good grief!" he cried, "what's wrong?"

"Just look at that horrid mallet up there, husband," moaned the mother. "Supposing our dear daughter was to marry the young squire, and supposing they was to have a child, and supposing the child was to come down here someday and draw the cider for supper, and supposing the mallet was to fall on his head and kill him! That would be dreadful!"

"My grandchild? Killed by a mallet? That would be awful!" said the father, and sat himself down and started a-crying, too.

Now, upstairs the young squire was getting impatient for his supper; so he came downstairs to see for himself what was going on. And there he found them, sitting side by side, crying their eyes out, with the floor all flooded with cider. So, the first thing he did was to turn off the tap on the cider cask. Then he said:

"What on earth is wrong with all of you, sitting here crying and letting good cider run all over the floor?"

They all three began to speak at once—"What if you was married, and you had a child and supposing the child was to come down here some day and draw the cider for supper, and supposing the mallet was to fall on his head and kill him? How dreadful that would be!" And they all cried and cried.

The young squire burst out laughing, and laughed and laughed until he was tired. But at last he reached up, took down the mallet, and put it safely on the floor. He shook his head and said, "I've travelled far and I've travelled fast, but never, *never*, have I met three such sillies as you. Now, I can't marry one of the three biggest sillies in the world. So I shall start again on my travels, and if I can find three bigger sillies than you three, then I'll come back and be married—not otherwise."

So he wished them all goodbye, and started again on his travels. And all three began to cry again; this time because the marriage was off!

Well, the young man travelled far and he travelled fast, but he never did find a bigger silly, until one day he came upon an old woman's cottage that had some grass growing up on the roof.

And the old woman was trying her best to drive a cow into going up a ladder to eat the grass on the roof. But the poor cow was afraid, and wouldn't go. Then the woman tried coaxing the cow, but it still wouldn't go. You never saw such a sight! The cow kept getting more and more flustered and obstinate, and the old woman angrier and angrier.

At last the young squire said, "Excuse me, but it would be much easier if you went up the ladder, cut the grass, and threw it down for the cow to eat."

"A likely story," said the old woman, "a cow can cut grass for herself. And the foolish thing will be quite safe up there, for I'll tie a rope around her neck, pass the rope down the chimney, and fasten the other end to my wrist. Then, while I'm doing the washing, she can't fall off without my knowing it. So, young sir, mind your own business."

Well, after awhile the old woman coaxed and cudgelled and bullied and badgered the cow into going up the ladder, and when she got it on the roof, she tied a rope around its neck and passed it down the chimney, and fastened the other end to her wrist. Then, she went about her washing, and the young squire went on his way. But he hadn't gone but a little way down the road when he heard the awfullest commotion. He rode back and discovered that the cow had fallen off the roof and got strangled by the rope around its neck, and that the weight of it had pulled the old woman halfway up the chimney where she got stuck and was covered with soot.

"That," said the young squire to himself, "was one bigger silly—now for two more."

He did not find one, however, until one night when he came upon a little inn. The inn was so full that he had to share a room with another traveller. His roommate proved to be quite a pleasant fellow, and after a nice chat, each slept well in his bed.

But the next morning when they were dressing—what does the stranger do, but carefully hang his trousers on the knobs of the dresser.

"What are you doing?" asked the young squire.

"I'm putting on my trousers," answered the stranger, and with that, went to the other side of the room, took a running leap, and tried to jump into his trousers.

But he didn't succeed, and took another leap. And so another and another and another until he got quite hot and bothered. And all the time the squire was laughing fit to split, for never in his life had he seen anything so comical.

The stranger stopped awhile and mopped his face with a handkerchief, for he was all in a sweat. "It's very easy for you to laugh," he said, "but trousers are the most awkwardest things to put on. It takes me the best part of the morning to get dressed. How do you manage yours?"

The young squire showed him the proper way to put on trousers, (as well as he could for laughing,) and the stranger was ever so grateful and said that he never would have thought of it.

"That," said the squire, "is a second bigger silly."

But he travelled far and he travelled fast without finding the third, until one night when the moon was shining right overhead, and he came upon a little village. Outside the village was a pond, and round about the pond there was a great crowd of villagers. Some had rakes, some had pitchforks, and some had brooms. They all were busy as busy, shouting out, raking, and sweeping away at the pond.

"What is the matter?" cried the squire, "has someone fallen in?"

"Matter enough," says they, "can't you see how the moon's fallen in the pond, and we can't get it out?"

And with that they set again to raking and forking and sweeping away.

The young squire burst out laughing, and told them they were fools for their pains, and bade them look up over their heads where the moon was shining, broad and full. But they wouldn't and couldn't believe it was only a reflection in the pond. And when he insisted, they began to abuse him, and threatened to give him a good soaking for his trouble. So he got on his horse, and made away as quickly as he could, leaving them all raking and forking and sweeping away. And for all we know they may be at it yet!

But the young squire said to himself, "There are many more sillies in the world than I thought; so there's nothing left to do but go back and marry the farmer's daughter. After all, she is no sillier than the rest."

And so they were married, and if they didn't live happily ever after, that's nothing to do with this story.

Beauty and the Beast

THERE was once a merchant who had three daughters. He was a very rich man who owned a fleet of ships that travelled around the world, seeking jewels and silks, and gold. From time to time, the ships would meet together at one port in order to sell and exchange their various cargoes.

It so happened that when, on one occasion, they had assembled for this purpose in the Persian Gulf, a terrible storm arose, and all of the merchant's ships were lost. In a single night he was reduced from riches to poverty.

No longer could he live in a noble palace, but in a small cottage; no longer could he keep servants to wait upon his every need. But he was still very fortunate, for his youngest daughter, whom everyone called Beauty, still loved him dearly, and tried to do all that she could to make his life as happy as it had been before.

She was called Beauty because of this great loveliness. For she was not only pretty, but charming and kind. She was beloved by all who met her. Her elder sisters, on the other hand, were vain, haughty, and unkind. As long as their voices were not heard, and their behaviour not seen, everyone thought they too, were beautiful, but their beauty seemed to vanish once people got to know them.

Beauty soon forgot her sadness at their losses, and found herself most content to live in the cottage. In fact, she seemed even better-natured than before.

But her contentment was not shared by her sisters. They were very sulky and sullen about the whole thing, and refused to help with any of the work in the house, leaving everything for poor Beauty to do. Because they were so unhappy, it showed up on their faces, and before long they were wrinkled from frowning, and the corners of their mouths turned down with peevishness. After a time, they grew positively ugly, while Beauty grew prettier by reason of her cheerfulness.

She had always loved flowers, and when they came to live in the cottage she planted a small garden. It grew to be more beautiful than any they had owned when they were wealthy, and all sorts of flowers grew there with the exception of roses. Strange to say, though she had tried her best to grow them, and planted many kinds, they always vanished the next night. At first they thought the little garden was being robbed, and set a watch, but again the roses vanished, and no robber was ever seen. Beauty wondered much at the disappearance of her roses, but her sisters laughed, and even accused her of trying to play a trick. So at last, Beauty grew tired of losing her roses, and gave up planting them altogether.

After the merchant and his daughters had lived in the cottage for nearly a year, news was brought to them of the safe arrival, in a distant port, of some of his most precious cargoes thought to be lost in the great storm. It was necessary for the merchant to go and claim his ship, and he resolved to set out that very day to that purpose.

His eldest daughters were overcome with joy at the news, yet Beauty remained quiet. While she was glad, she had grown so contented with her lot that she did not welcome another change.

"Tell me, daughters," said the merchant, "what presents would you have me bring for you upon my return?"

His eldest daughter asked for jewels, and a diamond watch that played exquisite music, bracelets studded with cameos, and pearls the size of walnuts.

But her sister broke in, "Stop, sister," she cried, "you will ruin our poor father before it comes to my turn. My wishes are not so extravagant. I will only ask for splendid Persian turbans, three dresses of the richest point lace, a variety of cashmere shawls, and a tortoise shell cabinet to hold them all." She paused, as though she were trying to think of something else, when the merchant turned to Beauty and said:

"Well, Beauty, what shall your present be?"

"I wish for nothing, Father, but your safe return."

"Ah, no Beauty, you must have some request."

Beauty thought for a moment and then she began to smile. "Well, then, dearest Father, as roses won't grow in my garden, bring me a rose, if one should come your way."

Her sisters laughed out loud at Beauty's request, but her father only smiled, and promised her the rose.

The next day the merchant started on his journey. Beauty was in tears at his departure. But not her sisters, who could not suppress their joy at the prospect of their presents.

The merchant travelled far, and arrived safely in port, and found his vessel richer even than he had hoped. He arranged his business, purchased all that his daughters had wished for, and began his journey home. Toward evening, he came to a wood. His horse turned down the path and made its way through the pine and cedars that lined the road. The evening was oppressive and dark, and as the sun set it bathed the wood in a crimson light. The stillness of the wood was almost painful, and before long the merchant became so lost in his thoughts of home that he forgot to guide his horse and left him to his own way.

The forest grew darker and gloomier, and the merchant went on, as if lost in a dream. Thunder sounded, and grey clouds folded one on the other, filling up the amber-tinted sky. Huge drops of rain fell upon the merchant before he realized where he was, and found that he was far from the road, and truly lost. Should he turn to the right? he asked himself. Should he go on or turn back? On all sides the forest was dark and impenetrable. Up came the thunder—roaring, Crash! Crash! as though the heavens were split with the sound. Long streaks of lightning flooded the forest with an eerie light, and the branches of the trees swayed like huge black plumes in the wind.

The merchant's horse was nearly blinded with fear, and refused to go on. The merchant, too, was terrified and did not know which way to turn to get out of the terrible forest.

When the thunder quieted, he heard a sweet sound, urging him on through the forest:

"On!" the voice said, "On! Thy journey's nearly done." And at that instant, a small blue light shone through the trees. The merchant took heart and spurred his horse in the direction of the light. When they were nearly there, the light expanded into a soft blue flame and all at once, it disappeared. In its place there was a sign that read:

Enter without fear. All are welcome here!

The merchant saw then that he stood at the gate of a magnificent castle. He pressed himself against the golden gate, and it opened before him without a noise. He passed beneath a marble arch and heard a sounding of trumpets, but still could not see anyone. He dismounted from his horse, which went right away to the door of the stable, as though it knew the way. The merchant crossed the courtyard and entered a long passageway. He passed a door and it sprang open into a beautiful dressing room where there waited dry clothes and a blazing fire. The merchant went in and lay down on the couch, exhausted from his journey. But he hesitated to touch anything until he heard a voice say to him:

> *"You're a guest for the night,*
> *And all that is right*
> *Will appear in your sight*
> *To be used without fright."*

He bathed himself in a basin of scented water, and changed into the fine clothes that awaited him. From there he went into a dining hall, and found a splendid meal ready for him to enjoy. Each time he finished a dish, it was removed by invisible hands, and replaced with something more delicious than the last. While he ate, he heard exquisite music, and when he was done he was guided by a light into a fine bedroom. Glad to have come to such a wonderful place, he fell into a sweet and refreshing sleep.

The next morning was beautiful and bright, and the merchant woke to find everything ready for his breakfast and journey. After breakfast, he walked in the gardens, and the flowers made him think of Beauty and how she longed for a rose. He gazed around and at last found some roses growing on a vine.

He had just plucked a crimson blossom when a monster seized him by the neck.

"Ungrateful wretch!" it cried. "Is this the way you repay my kindness? I have given you shelter and comfort and in return you steal my roses! You will die for this!"

The merchant trembled in the monster's grasp. "My lord," he said—"my lord—"

"I am not your lord," roared the monster. "Call me as I am—call me Beast!"

"Pardon me then—Beast. I did not know you would mind."

"Were the roses yours?" The merchant gave no reply.

"Answer me!" roared the Beast.

The merchant stood silent, not wanting the Beast to know the reason for his taking the rose.

"It was your youngest daughter asked for the rose! I know all, Merchant. And since you were ready to suffer for her sake, I will spare your life. Take your presents home, but you must return here in one week, or send someone in your place. Take your rose and go."

The merchant stooped to pick up the rose which had fallen from his hand, and when he turned to thank him, the monster was nowhere to be found. The rose seemed to wilt at once, but the merchant placed it in his pocket and proceeded on his journey home. His horse seemed to move so fast its hooves barely touched the ground, and they galloped for many miles before they were clear of the forest. It was almost evening by the time the merchant reached his cottage door.

When he approached the cottage, Beauty ran to meet him, her face shining with happiness. But then she saw how sad her father looked, and asked, "Why, Father, why so sad? Tell me, what has happened?"

Her father related his terrible tale, and when he was done, he took the withered rose from his pocket and said, "Here child, enjoy the simple gift you asked for."

Beauty took the rose from his fingers, and it instantly began to revive, growing fresh and crimson in her hands. "Oh, Father," she cried, "you must not be unhappy. It was for my sake that this has happened, and so it will be me who will return to the Beast's castle."

Her father protested, but she stood firm. "No matter what the monster has in store, I will go. Besides, Father, your life is more important than mine—if you were to die, who would care for my sisters?"

The two sisters came running out and without so much as greeting him, demanded of their father the presents he had brought. Beauty asked them to leave him alone, for his heart was heavy, and when she told them the story of the rose, they turned on her saying:

"You wicked girl, to ask for a rose. See all the trouble you've caused? The Beast might have taken our jewels and clothes, had he known of them!" And with that, they began to shout at her, and chase her, trying to take away her rose. But every time they got near it, the flower seemed to drift away from them, staying safe in Beauty's grasp. Then their father commanded them to be silent, and never to speak of the rose again.

At last the morning came for their departure. Beauty gave all she had to her sisters, and kissed them goodbye. And though they pretended to be sad, they were really glad to see her go, for they were very jealous of her. The merchant insisted that he would ride with her, and see her safely to the castle, and so they mounted their horses and set off. As soon as they arrived at the forest, the merchant's horse darted into the wood, as though it knew the path, and Beauty followed, thinking that she had never seen a wood so grand and beautiful. The nightingales sang softly to her, the air filled with scents of flowers and pines, and a tiny troop of butterflies formed around her horse's head, and led her down the path.

At last they reached the palace gate, and Beauty read the sign.

Enter without fear, for all are welcome here!

The golden gates flew open, and Beauty's horse placed itself in front of some marble steps with golden rails, so that she might dismount more easily. Her father too, dismounted, and they passed into a great hall. The palace seemed to him to be even more beautiful than it had been on his last visit, and he was pleased that the Beast had thought to provide for his daughter's every need.

At last the moment came for the two to part, and they did so, weeping with love for one another. But Beauty urged her father to go for his own safety, lest the Beast be angered that they both had come. And so the merchant left, and rode off into the wood, certain he was never to see her again.

Beauty was heartsick at being alone, and wandered through the palace. She came upon a beautiful sign that said: 'Beauty's Apartment' and inside found the most exquisite things she could have asked for: velvet chairs; great, thick, carpets, and footstools made of gold. The curtains were made of satin and powdered with stars, and there were hangings of the finest lace. There was a library in one room, in another musical instruments of every imaginable kind, in another materials for needlework. Adjoining this were her dressing and bedrooms. She entered the former, and found numberless dresses, more beautiful than she had ever laid eyes on. Yet, she lacked the courage to touch anything, and sat down listlessly. She raised her drooping eyes, and saw a wonderful, transparent cloth floating before her. And on it were inscribed the words:

> *"Welcome Beauty, Do not fear.*
> *You are Queen and Mistress here!*
> *Speak your wishes, speak your will,*
> *And your desires shall be fulfilled."*

Beauty tried to resign herself to her fate, and was truly grateful that if she was to be separated from those she loved, at least she was intended to be comfortable. She wandered out into the dining hall, and there found a magnificent feast prepared from all that she liked best to eat. She sat down and began her meal, each course set and removed by invisible hands. During the dinner exquisite music was performed, and she smiled for the first time since coming to the castle.

Then, a magic flute sounded a few bars of music, and a voice said:

> *"The Beast is near,*
> *And asks leave to appear."*

Beauty was terribly afraid, and yet was determined not to show it. She called out: "Enter Beast, if that is your will."

A door sprang open, and the Beast entered. And though she tried with all her will, Beauty could not help but hide her face at his ugliness.

When he spoke, the Beast's voice was kind and musical. "Do not be afraid, Beauty, for I shall not harm you. Be assured that my palace and all its contents are yours to command. You have but to wish for something, and it shall appear before you. And now, since my presence is distasteful to you, I shall withdraw."

Beauty thanked him for his kindness, but dared not raise her head.

And so for a time Beauty lived alone in the castle, but for the unseen musicians, who played her favourite music, and all the other invisible creatures who saw to her every wish. She found the gardens the most beautiful of all, and spent many happy hours wandering among the flowers and trees.

Yet she was lonely, and began to long for some company, and though she tried wishing, none appeared.

One evening as she sat in the garden, she heard again the magic flute and the voice that said:

> *"The Beast is near*
> *And asks leave to appear."*

She started with happiness at the prospect of someone to talk to. She said, "Appear Beast!" and though she shuddered at his approach, he did not seem so ugly as before, and she was glad when he stayed to converse with her.

After that, he came to see her every evening, and she found that as the days passed, she grew fond of him, in spite of his ugliness.

One evening, as the two sat underneath the rose arbour, Beast took her hand gently into his own. "Beauty," he said, "will you marry me?"

Beauty started up from her place—terrified. "I can never marry you!" she cried, "You are a beast!"

The moment she had uttered these words, she could have bitten her tongue, but there was no help for it, for the Beast hung his head in sorrow, and left without a word.

The next night, Beauty waited for him but he did not come, nor the next night after that. Beauty listened anxiously for the sounds of the flute, yet there were no sweet notes to be heard. "What can this mean?" she asked herself. "Will Beast never appear again? I am so sorry that I have hurt him. I would not mind if he were a thousand times more ugly, if only he would come and see me once again."

She had scarcely time to finish her thought before the flute sounded and the Beast appeared.

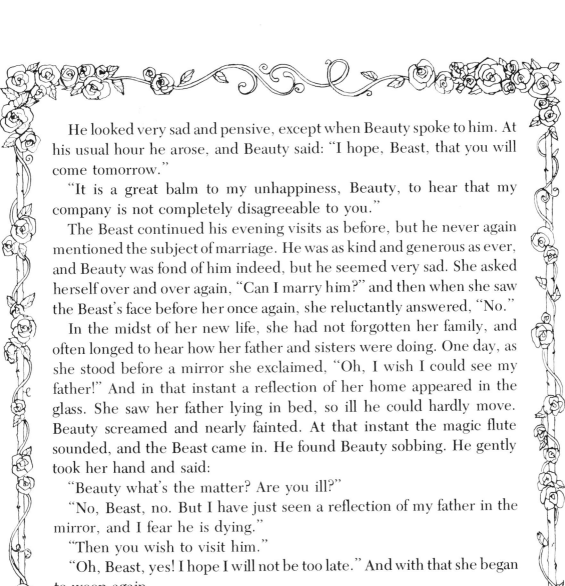

He looked very sad and pensive, except when Beauty spoke to him. At his usual hour he arose, and Beauty said: "I hope, Beast, that you will come tomorrow."

"It is a great balm to my unhappiness, Beauty, to hear that my company is not completely disagreeable to you."

The Beast continued his evening visits as before, but he never again mentioned the subject of marriage. He was as kind and generous as ever, and Beauty was fond of him indeed, but he seemed very sad. She asked herself over and over again, "Can I marry him?" and then when she saw the Beast's face before her once again, she reluctantly answered, "No."

In the midst of her new life, she had not forgotten her family, and often longed to hear how her father and sisters were doing. One day, as she stood before a mirror she exclaimed, "Oh, I wish I could see my father!" And in that instant a reflection of her home appeared in the glass. She saw her father lying in bed, so ill he could hardly move. Beauty screamed and nearly fainted. At that instant the magic flute sounded, and the Beast came in. He found Beauty sobbing. He gently took her hand and said:

"Beauty what's the matter? Are you ill?"

"No, Beast, no. But I have just seen a reflection of my father in the mirror, and I fear he is dying."

"Then you wish to visit him."

"Oh, Beast, yes! I hope I will not be too late." And with that she began to weep again.

"Take the rose which your father first gathered. As long as you keep it with you, you have but to wish for something and it will be yours."

"Oh, Beast, thank you!"

"I have only one condition to make, you must return within a week. Take care that you are not away longer than that. Even that time will appear like years to me."

"You may rely on me, Beast."

The Beast took her hand and pressed it to his lips. "Goodbye, Beauty, goodbye."

When the Beast had gone, Beauty took the rose and pressed it to her heart. "I wish to be at home," she said, and no sooner had she uttered the words than she found herself on the porch outside her father's cottage. She knocked on the door, and it was opened by her eldest sister, who was very surprised to see her and said:

"Why Beauty, we thought you dead. Sister and I were sure you had been eaten by your monster long ago."

Beauty ignored her unkind greeting, and fell into her sister's arms, weeping with happiness. "How is my father?" she said, "Is he alive?"

"Yes, and much better, no thanks to you—we thought you had forgotten us!"

"Never, never" cried Beauty, "I came as soon as I heard he was ill."

"Well, go in and see him, then—since you've come."

Beauty found her father much better and both were joyful at seeing the other again. Beauty's presence hastened the recovery of the old man, and he became quite well again before she had been at home two days. He delighted in hearing all her news and the tales of the palace, and how kind the Beast was to her. Hearing of the wonders of the palace made her sisters quite jealous, and they plotted between themselves as to how they might take Beauty's place there. The eldest began to think of ways that she might steal Beauty's rose, so that her own wishes might be fulfilled.

One night as Beauty slept, she took it from her, and wished herself at the Beast's palace, but the instant she touched it, the flower withered, and instead of being transported to the palace the girl was plumped down into the pigsty, rolling around in the mud. She roared for someone to come and help her, and when some farmers came to take her out, she cast aside the rose, and refused to tell anyone how she got there.

Beauty was due to return to the palace, and when the week was up she looked for her rose, and found it was gone. When she found that she had lost her way to keep her promise to Beast she grew anxious and sad. Her sister saw her grief, but refused to tell her where the rose was, that she might return.

She searched and searched, and the day passed. She began to think that the affair of the pigsty might have something to do with its disappearance, but could not bring herself to accuse her sister of such treachery. She wandered unhappily over the grounds, and when all at once, in the last light of the evening, she spied the rose on top of a pile of rubbish, nearly withered. Hastily she took it up, and bade her father and sisters farewell. She wished herself at once back at the palace, and in the blink of an eye was back in her own room. She looked anxiously for the Beast but he was nowhere to be found. She sat up all night long, but still he did not come. At last she fell asleep, certain that he would appear in the morning, but when he did not, she took to wandering from room to room, calling for him. But she could not find him, and in despair she took up the rose, and wished herself in the Beast's presence. She was horrified! He lay as if dead. She felt that his heart was still beating, and ran to a pool for some water. As she bathed his face, he uttered a groan, and feebly opened one eye.

"Beauty," he said, "Did you return only to see me die? I could not have believed you would have lied to me. It was impossible for me to live without you. But I am glad to see you once before I die."

Beauty began to weep uncontrollably. "Oh Beast, do not die. What can I do to save you?"

"Will you marry me?" faintly murmured the Beast.

"Willingly," Beauty answered. "For I truly love you."

She covered her face and wept. But when she opened her eyes again, she saw not the Beast, but one of the handsomest princes she had ever seen.

"I have been enchanted," said the Prince, "condemned by a spiteful fairy to live as a Beast until I found one who would marry me for myself, regardless of my beastly form. I was helped by another fairy, who gave me the rose tree and told me it would be the means of releasing me from the spell."

Beauty fell happily into his arms, and they walked out into the palace which seemed at once to be filled with music and bustling with people. There she found her father, who had been invited to the wedding, but not her sisters, who had been changed into stone statues until they reformed themselves.

And so it was Beauty and the Prince were married and lived to a happy old age.

The Golden Goose

THERE was once a man who had three sons, the youngest of which was called Dummling. One day, the old man told his eldest son to pack himself a lunch and go into the forest to cut some wood. He went along into the wood, and worked very hard all morning. When he stopped at midday to have his lunch, a little old grey man came along and said:

"May I have a crust of bread and a glass of milk? I am faint with hunger and very thirsty."

But the son said, "If I give you some, I won't have enough for myself."

It seems the little grey man had magical powers, and when he heard that, he decided that anyone so unkind should get what they deserved. And that is the reason why, when the selfish boy set to work again, his axe slipped and he cut himself, and was obliged to go home to have his leg bandaged.

And so it happened that the second son had to take his brother's place and go into the forest to finish the job. He too, met the little old man, and the man asked him if he would spare a bit of bread and milk.

"If I give away all my lunch to the likes of you, I won't have enough for myself," the second son answered him. "Be off with you!"

The little old man went off, muttering under his breath. "You will be wiser when you've hurt yourself," he said. The second son went back to work, and before long the axe slipped and he cut himself in the leg.

Then Dummling begged to be allowed to go and finish the wood cutting. But his father told him, "Your brothers, who are far cleverer than you, have only come to harm by it. You had better stay home."

But Dummling gave his father no peace until at last he allowed him to go into the forest.

His mother gave him a cake mixed with water and baked in the ashes, and a bottle of sour beer. When Dummling reached the forest, he met the little grey man.

"Give me something to eat and drink; I am so hungry and thirsty," he said.

Dummling answered him. "I have only an ash cake and a bottle of sour beer," he said. "But I will be most glad to share with you." So they sat down to eat. But when Dummling pulled out the cake, it was a nice sweet cake, and the bottle of sour beer had turned to cold, fresh milk.

The little grey man said, "Since you have a kind heart, and are willing to share what you have, I will give you good luck. There stands an old tree. Cut it down and you will find something at the roots." And with that, the little grey man disappeared altogether.

Dummling cut down the tree, and when it fell—lo and behold—there was a goose sitting among the roots, its feathers made of the purest gold.

He took it in his arms, and made his way out of the forest.

He came to an inn, where he stopped to spend the night on his way home. The landlord of the place had three daughters, and when they saw the beautiful goose, they felt they must have one of its feathers. So, they waited until Dummling had fallen asleep, and the eldest of them stole up and tried to pluck a feather from the beautiful golden goose. But no

sooner had she laid hands upon it than she was stuck fast, and no amount of pulling and tugging could free her. The second sister tried her best to help, but no sooner did she touch her sister than she too, was stuck. And so it was with the third.

In the morning, Dummling took up the goose and went on his way, paying no attention to three who hung on behind, tripping and falling over one another. Before long, a clergyman came along the road, and seeing the three girls cried, "Girls shouldn't run after young men like that!" But when he went up to lead the youngest girl away, no sooner had he touched her than he was stuck fast to her hand.

Soon after that, the clergyman's assistant came along and was very disturbed to see him trailing along like that.

"Sir," he said, "where do you think you're going? Have you forgotten there is a wedding today?" And when the clergyman paid no attention, the man went and took hold of his sleeve. And you know what happened then.

After a walk down the road, they came across a couple of men digging a ditch. The clergyman and his assistant called to them to come and get them unstuck, but no sooner had the two tried, than they were stuck as tight as the rest. And so the seven trailed along after Dummling and his golden goose, with he paying not the slightest mind to any of them.

Before long, they came to a land where there lived a Princess who had never laughed. Her father, the King, thought this a great tragedy, and so put out a proclamation saying that any who could make the solemn Princess laugh could marry her and rule half the kingdom.

When Dummling heard this, he took along the goose and the seven who trailed along behind him, straight to the King's palace. When they were brought before the Princess and she saw them all stumbling along, tripping on the other's heels, she laughed until it seemed as though she would never stop. So, Dummling married her, and she has not gone a day without laughing since.

But what became of the golden goose, and all those who were stuck on behind, no one ever did find out.

Rumpelstiltskin

ONCE there was a miller who was very poor, but had one beautiful daughter. It happened one day that he had occasion to speak to the King, and, in order to give himself importance, he told him that he had a daughter who was not only very pretty, but that she could spin straw into gold.

"That," said the King, "is an art I would like to see. Bring the girl to my castle, and there I will put her to the test."

The miller did as he was told, and escorted his daughter to the castle that very evening. There she was led to a room filled with straw and given a spindle and wheel. The King then said to her: "If you fail to spin this straw into gold by morning you will die." He then shut and locked the door himself, and left the poor girl there alone.

And because the miller's daughter could not for the life of her figure out how it was that one spun straw into gold, she began to weep. Before long, a little man opened the door, tipped his hat and said:

"Good evening, miller's daughter, why is it that you weep so?"

"The King has ordered me to spin straw into gold, and I don't know how!" she answered him, and began to weep again.

The little man squinted up his eyes and said, "What will you give me if I spin it for you?"

"I have very little to give," said the miller's daughter. "But there is my necklace."

The little man took the necklace and sat down before the wheel. Whirr, whirr, whirr—before the girl's eyes, he spun the straw into gold. He went on and on through the night, until at last the room was filled to the rafters with gold.

The little man, when he was finished, tipped his hat to her and left.

At sunrise, the King came in and exclaimed over her night's work. But he was a very greedy king, who could not get enough of gold, and so led her to an even bigger room filled with straw and told her:

"As you value your life, you must spin all this into gold tonight."

With that, he left her, and she sat down to weep. Once again, the little man opened the door, tipped his hat to her and said:

"Miller's daughter, what will you give me if I spin this into gold?"

"The ring from my finger," she answered him.

The little man took the ring, and sat down to spin. Whirr, whirr, whirr—before her eyes, the straw was once again being spun into gold. And by the next morning, the room was filled to the rafters with gold. When the King came in and saw this marvel, he was happier than he had ever been, but since he could never have enough gold, he led the girl to yet another room even bigger than the last and said:

"You must spin this too, in one night, but if you succeed, you will become my wife." For he thought: She may be only a miller's daughter, but there is certainly no richer woman in the world.

As soon as the girl was left alone, the little man appeared, and said:

"Miller's daughter, what will you give me if I spin this for you?"

143

"I have nothing else to give—" she answered him.

"Then you must promise to give me the first child you have after you become Queen."

"Who knows what will happen?" the miller's daughter thought, and since she could think of no other way out of her difficulty, she promised him what he asked. And so the little man began to spin, never stopping until all the straw was spun into gold. And when the King came in the morning and saw that she had done as he asked, he decided to marry her that very day. And the pretty miller's daughter became a queen.

In a year's time, the Queen brought a fine child into the world, and the whole kingdom rejoiced. She had forgotten all about the little man, until one day he appeared before her and said:

"Give me what you promised me."

The Queen was terrified, and offered the little man all the riches of her kingdom, if only he would leave the child; but he said, "No. I would rather have something living than all treasures of the world."

Then the Queen began to weep and lament until the little man took pity on her. He said: "I will give you three days, and if at the end of that time, you still have not guessed my name, you must give up the child."

The Queen spent the whole night thinking up all the names she had ever heard, and when the little man came the next day, she asked him:

"Is it Caspar, Melchior, or Balthazar?"

"No," said the little man, giggling with glee. "That is not my name."

And so she went through all the names she knew, but after each, he giggled and said, "No that is not my name."

The next day, the Queen sent out a messenger over all the kingdom to inquire about all the most unusual names, and when the little man came again, she asked him, "Is your name Cowribs? Or Spiderlegs? Or Spindleshanks?"

But after each, the little man shook head and said, "No, no—that's not it—that's not my name."

On the third day, the Queen's messenger came back and said that he had not heard anything unusual or new in the way of names. "But," he said, "as I passed through the woods, I came to a little knoll, and near it was a little house. Before the house there burned a fire, and the most comical little man danced round it, singing:

> '*Today I do the baking, Tomorrow I brew my beer.*
> *The day after that, the Queen's child comes in.*
> *Oh! I am glad there none who's here*
> *That knows my name is Rumpelstiltskin!'*

The Queen was pleased beyond words at hearing that, and the next day, when the little man came in she said:

"Now, my pretty Queen, what is my name?"

"Is it Jack?" she asked him.

"No," he answered her.

"Is it Tom?"

"No," said the little man, "that's not it, either."

"Are you by chance called Rumpelstiltskin?" asked the Queen.

"The devil told you that, the devil told you that!" screamed the little man, and in a rage he stamped his foot so hard it went right into the ground up to his knee. Then, in his fury he seized his other foot with both hands, and split himself in two. And that was the end of him.

The Sleeping Beauty
in the Wood

THERE were formerly a King and Queen, who were sorry that they had never had a child; so sorry that it cannot be told. They tried all ways, and travelled all around the world for an answer, but to no avail.

At last, however, the Queen had a daughter. There was a great christening, and the little Princess had for her godmothers all the fairies they could find in the whole kingdom. They found seven of them, and from each the little Princess would receive a fine gift, as was the custom of fairies in those days. By this means, then, the Princess was granted every perfection.

After the christening, the whole kingdom returned to the palace, where there was prepared a great feast for the fairies. The King placed before each of them a magnificent cover made of gold, and inside there was a spoon, a knife, and a fork, also made of gold and studded with the rarest diamonds and rubies. But as they were all sitting down, there came into the hall a very old fairy, whom they had not thought to invite, because it had been over fifty years since she had been out of a certain tower, and everyone thought she was either dead or enchanted.

The King ordered that a place be set for her as well, but he had no golden setting to offer, because there had only been seven made. The old fairy fancied that she had been slighted, and was heard to mutter threats between her teeth. One of the young fairies who sat nearby heard her grumbling, and thought she might give the little Princess an unlucky gift. And so when they rose from the table, she went to hide herself behind the curtains, so that she would be the last to speak, and might in some way be able to repair the evil the old fairy intended.

All the other fairies began to give the Princess their gifts. The youngest said that she would be the most beautiful person in the world; the next, that she would have the wit of an angel; the third, that she should be entirely graceful; the fourth, that she should dance wonderfully well; the fifth, that she would sing like a nightingale; and the sixth, that she would play all kinds of music to perfection.

The old fairy's turn came next, and, her head shaking with spite and age, she promised that the Princess should pierce her hand with a spindle and die of the wound. The whole palace cried out at this and fell to weeping.

At that instant, the young fairy came from behind the curtain and said: "Do not worry, oh, King and Queen. Your daughter shall not die of this disaster. While I have no power to undo all that which my elder has done, I can promise you that the Princess shall not die from her wound, but instead will fall into a deep sleep, one that will last a hundred years. And at the end of that time, a King's son will come to awaken her."

But the King, in order to prevent this terrible thing, immediately ordered that all the spindles in the kingdom be burned, and that spinning by anyone was forbidden forever after in his land.

Fifteen or sixteen years passed, and the Princess grew to be the most beautiful and graceful creature that ever was. One day, when the King and Queen were out, the Princess was amusing herself by running up and down all the stairs in the palace, and singing to herself for company. Before long, she came to a little staircase that led to a tiny tower room. There sat an old, old, woman spinning at her wheel. In fact, the woman was so ancient, and had been sitting so long, that she had never heard of the King's proclamation. The Princess bowed to her and asked, "What are you doing here?"

"Why," the old woman answered, "I am spinning."

"It is very pretty–looking. May I try it?"

She had no sooner taken it into her hand than, whether it was because of the old fairy's curse or not, it pierced her finger and she fell down in a faint. The old woman did not know what to do, and called out to the rest of the palace for help. And though they rushed to the Princess' aid and

tried all ways to revive her, she stayed in her swoon and would not awaken.

The King and Queen returned, and when they saw what had come to pass, they were reminded of the old fairy's curse, and when they had made sure that she breathed, and saw that she had only fallen into a deep sleep, they ordered that the Princess be carried to the finest bedchamber in the palace and laid on a bed embroidered in silver and gold.

She might have been an angel sleeping there—so beautiful was she. Her cheeks were coral coloured; her lips carnation, and her golden hair spread out across the silver pillow as she slept. The King ordered that she was not to be disturbed, but allowed to sleep away the time until her hour of awakening should come.

He sent word to the young fairy—who returned from a far corner of the world in a flaming chariot drawn by dragons. The King himself helped her from the chariot, and when she saw what he had done, she approved it at once, but she had great foresight. She knew that when the Princess awakened after one hundred years, she would not know what to do with herself, and this is what she did:

With her wand she touched everything in the palace so that it would sleep with her, governesses, maids-in-waiting, gentlemen, officers, stewards, cooks, scullions, guards, pages, footmen—all. Likewise she touched all the horses in the stables, the great dogs in the courtyard, and even little Mopsey, the Princess's spaniel who slept at the foot of her bed.

And at once they all fell asleep, so that they might not awake before their mistress, and might be ready to serve her when she awoke. All this was done in a moment, for fairies are never long in doing their business.

The King and Queen kissed their daughter goodbye, and went out of the palace, issuing a proclamation that none should come near it. But that was unnecessary, for as soon as they left, the fairy caused a great number of rose trees to grow up around the place, and at once they entwined together, bushes and briars, leaves and blossoms until neither man nor beast could pass through the hedge, and nothing but the great tower could be seen from all around.

A hundred years passed, and Beauty slept on. It so happened that one day a young Prince was out hunting, and came upon the extraordinary place, and when he returned he asked any who might know:

"Whose towers are those, in the middle of the wood?"

The people answered him as best they might.

"It is a haunted castle, only spirits dwell there," or they said:

"That is where the conjurors and witches go to have their meetings."

Most believed that an ogre lived there, and the reason no one knew of him for certain was that he had eaten all his visitors, and no one had come back to tell the tale.

Just then a very old man came up to the Prince and said: "If you please, Your Highness, it is fifty years since I heard the story from my father, who, in his turn, heard it from my grandfather. They say there is a beautiful Princess who dwells up there, and that she is enchanted, and must sleep a hundred years before a Prince should come and awaken her."

The Prince was all on fire at this, certain that he was the one who might accomplish the deed. And without further hesitation, he resolved to go and rescue the beautiful Princess from her long sleep.

He had barely approached the wood when the trees at once began to part themselves, allowing him to pass. He walked up to the castle and shuddered at the deathly quiet of the place. There were bodies all around; man and beast stretched out on the stairs and in the halls as if dead. But he pressed on. Young Princes are always brave.

He passed through many rooms, and there found all as before, gentlemen and ladies all asleep—some standing, some sitting. At last he came to a chamber, all gilded with gold, where sleeping peacefully, was the most beautiful sight he had ever beheld—a Princess so lovely as to seem almost unreal. He approached her and fell to his knees before her. Trembling, he leaned over her and brushed her cheek with his lips, that she might awaken.

And since the enchantment had at last come to an end, the Princess opened her beautiful eyes and looked at him tenderly saying,

"Is it you, my Prince? I have waited for you very long."

The Prince did not know how to show his joy at this, except to tell her that he loved her better than he did himself, and ask that she become his wife. The Princess was not in the least surprised by this, for the good fairy had promised her these things in her hundred years of dreaming, and so she had the time to think of what to say to him.

In the meantime, all the palace yawned and stretched and went about their business as though nothing unusual had happened. The chief lady of honour grew very impatient and called the Princess to supper, and the Prince helped her to rise from her bed. She was dressed magnificently, though the Prince took care not to tell her that she was dressed like his great-grandmother. But she was nonetheless beautiful and charming for all that. He led her out into the great hall of looking glasses, where they dined, and heard the music of the court musicians playing songs of a hundred years before.

And after they had feasted, the whole company assembled in the chapel and they were married in happiness, and lived to a great age.

The Princess
and the Pea

ONCE upon a time there was a prince who wanted a princess; but she would have to be a *real* princess. He travelled all around the world to find one, but each time he did, there was always something wrong. True, there were princesses enough, but he found it difficult to make out which were the *real* ones. So he came home again, and was very sad, for all he wanted in the world was to have a real princess for his own.

One evening a terrible storm came on; it thundered and it lightened, and the rain poured down in torrents. It was dreadful! Suddenly there was a knocking at the gate, and the Prince's father, the old King, went to open it.

It was a princess standing out there in the terrible weather. But oh, what a sight she was! The water ran from her hair and clothes; it ran down into the toes of her slippers and out at the heels. And yet she insisted she was a real princess.

"We'll soon find that out," thought the old Queen. But she said nothing at all, and went into the chamber where the Princess was to spend the night. There she took all the bedding off the bed, and laid a single pea at the bottom. Then she took twenty mattresses and laid them on top, and twenty eiderdown quilts on top of those. When the Princess came in to go to bed, she had to have a ladder to climb to the top of it all.

In the morning, the old King and Queen asked the girl how she had slept.

"Oh!" said she, "It was awful, I scarcely shut my eyes the whole night. Heaven knows what was in the bed, but it was so hard that I am fairly black and blue."

When they all heard that, they knew for certain she was a real princess, because she had felt the pea right through the twenty mattresses and the twenty more eiderdown quilts. Nobody but a real princess could be as sensitive as that.

So the Prince took her for his wife, for he now had found a real princess at last; and the pea was placed in an art museum, where it may still be seen, if no one has stolen it. There, that is a *real* story!

Rapunzel

THERE was once a man and his wife who had long wished in vain for a child, and at last they had reason to hope that heaven would grant their wish. There was a little window at the back of their house, which overlooked a beautiful garden full of lovely flowers and shrubs. It was, however, surrounded by a wall, and nobody dared to enter because it belonged to a witch who was feared by everybody.

One day the woman, standing at this window and looking into the garden, saw a bed planted with beautiful rampion. It looked so fresh and green that she longed to eat some of it. This longing increased every day; and as she knew it could never be satisfied, she began to look pale and miserable and to pine away. Her husband was alarmed and said, "What ails you, my dear wife?"

"Alas!" she answered. "If I cannot get any of the rampion to eat from the garden behind our house, I shall die."

Her husband, who loved her, thought, "Before you let your wife die you must fetch her some of that rampion, cost what it may." So in the twilight, he climbed over the wall into the witch's garden, hastily picked a handful of rampion, and took it back to his wife. She immediately prepared it and ate it very eagerly. It was so very, very, good that the next day her longing for it increased threefold. She could have no peace unless her husband fetched her some more. So in the twilight he set out again, but when he got over the wall he was terrified to see the witch before him.

"How dare you come into my garden like a thief and steal my rampion?" she said, with angry looks. "It shall be the worse for you!"

"Alas!" he answered. "Be merciful to me. I am only here because of necessity. My wife sees your rampion from the window, and she has such a longing for it that she would die if she could not get some of it."

The witch's anger faded and she said to him, "If it is as you say, I will allow you to take away with you as much rampion as you like, but on one condition. You must give me the child which your wife is about to bring into the world. I will care for it like a mother, and all will be well with it."

In his fear the man consented to everything. And when the baby was born, the witch appeared, gave it the name of Rapunzel, which means rampion, and took it away with her.

Rapunzel was the most beautiful child under the sun. When she was twelve years old, the witch shut her up in a tower which stood in a wood. It had neither staircase nor doors, but only a little window quite high up in the wall.

When the witch wanted to enter the tower, she stood at the foot of it and cried, "Rapunzel, Rapunzel, let down your hair!"

Rapunzel had splendid hair, as fine as spun gold and as long as a rope. As soon as she heard the voice of the witch, she unfastened her braids and twisted her hair round a hook by the window. It fell all the way down to the ground, and the witch climbed up by it.

It happened a couple of years later that the King's son rode through the forest and came close to the tower. As he passed by the tower, he heard a song so lovely that he stopped to listen. It was Rapunzel who, in her loneliness was singing to pass the time. The Prince wanted to join her, and he looked for the door of the tower but there was no door to find.

He rode home, but the song had touched his heart so deeply that he went into the forest every day to listen to it. Once when he was hidden behind a tree he saw a witch come to the tower and call out, "Rapunzel, Rapunzel, let down your golden hair!"

Then Rapunzel lowered her braids of hair and the witch climbed up to her. "If that is the ladder by which one ascends," he thought, "I will try my luck myself." And the next day, when it began to grow dark, he went to the tower and cried, "Rapunzel, Rapunzel, let down your golden hair!"

The hair fell down and the Prince climbed up it.

At first Rapunzel was terrified, for she had never set eyes on a man before. But he talked to her kindly, and told her that his heart had been so deeply touched by her song that he had had no peace and was obliged to see her. Then Rapunzel lost her fear. And when he asked her if she would have him for her husband, and she saw that he was young and handsome, she thought, "He will love me better than that old witch." So she said, "Yes," and laid her hand in his. She said, "I will gladly go with you, but I do not know how I am to get down from this tower. When you come, will you bring a skein of silk with you every time? I will twist it into a ladder, and when it is long enough I will descend by it, and you can take me away with you on your horse."

She arranged with him that he should come and see her every evening, for the old witch came in the daytime.

The witch discovered nothing till one day Rapunzel suddenly said to her, "Tell me, old witch, how can it be that you are so much heavier to draw up than the young Prince who will be here before long?"

"Oh, you wicked child, what do you say? I thought I had separated you from all the world, and yet you have deceived me." In her rage she seized Rapunzel's beautiful hair, twisted it round her left hand, snatched up a pair of shears, and cut off the braids, which fell to the ground. She was so merciless that she took poor Rapunzel away into a wilderness, where she forced her to live in the greatest grief and misery.

In the evening of the day on which she had banished Rapunzel, the witch fastened the braids which she had cut off to the hook by the window. And when the Prince came and called:

"Rapunzel, Rapunzel, let down your hair!"

—she lowered the hair. The Prince climbed up, but there he found, not his beloved Rapunzel, but the witch, who looked at him with angry and wicked eyes.

"Ah!" she cried mockingly, "You have come to fetch your lady love, but the pretty bird is no longer in her nest. And she can sing no more, for the cat has seized her and it will scratch your eyes, too. Rapunzel is lost to you. You will never see her again."

The Prince was beside himself with grief, and in his despair he sprang out of the window. He was not killed, but his eyes were scratched out by the thorns where he fell. He wandered blind in the wood and had nothing but roots and berries to eat. He did nothing but weep and lament over the loss of his beloved Rapunzel. In this way he wandered about for some years, till at last he reached the wilderness where Rapunzel had been living very sadly in great poverty.

He heard a voice which seemed very familiar to him and he went towards it. Rapunzel knew him at once and fell weeping upon his neck. Two of her tears fell upon his eyes, and they immediately were healed and he could see as well as ever.

He took her to his kingdom, where he was received with great joy, and they lived long and happily together.

The Sorcerer's Apprentice

A MAN who needed help in his workshop came upon a lad who seemed in need of a job.

"You look hungry, son. It so happens that I need an apprentice in my workshop. Can you read and write?"

"Yes, sir, indeed I can!" said the lad, who had set out to seek his fortune that very morning.

"Too bad, then, for I require an apprentice who cannot read and write."

"I beg your pardon, sir," said the lad hastily. "I really cannot read and write. I said I could only because I thought it would help me get the job."

"Excellent," said the man. "You've got the job. Come along to my workshop, and I'll set you to work."

Now, the lad knew perfectly well how to read and write, and he was suspicious of any man who had no use for such valuable skills. His suspicions deepened when he saw the workshop. It was as dark and musty as a cave. A giant copper cauldron bubbled on the hearth. The walls, dusty and cobwebby, held hundreds of books, great glass beakers, oddly shaped jars, and all sorts of queer scales and measuring devices. "Why, this man is a sorcerer!" said the lad to himself. "If I keep my eyes open, I might learn something useful."

Every day the lad did his chores. He stirred the foul-smelling brew that simmered in the cauldron. He ground up all manner of herbs. He fetched wood and kept the fire blazing in the hearth.

One night, when he was sure the sorcerer was asleep, the lad crept from his bed and carefully drew down a book from one of the shelves. Each page was covered with ancient spidery writing, mystic symbols, formulas, spells, and recipes for potions. Unable to put down the book, he read until dawn. Then, his head swimming with incantations, he crept back to bed.

The next night, the lad studied two more books, this time memorizing the formulas. Night after night, he read and studied. The more he learned, the more obvious it became to him that his employer was a wicked sorcerer.

Each day while the sorcerer was out—doing evil, no doubt—the lad practised casting spells. He turned a cat into a mouse, then back into a cat. He turned a broom into a cello and back again.

One day, the sorcerer came in early and caught him practising. "Lying wretch!" he cried. "So you can read and write! You've stolen my secrets!" With that, he moved to toss the lad into the boiling cauldron. The quick-witted apprentice immediately cast a spell and changed the sorcerer into a bird. But, as he flew out the door into the forest, the sorcerer uttered a stronger incantation and changed into a larger, faster bird.

Wings flapping, the sorcerer flew after his apprentice. Quick as a wink, the lad changed into a fish. Just as quickly, the sorcerer became a bigger fish. Then the boy became a gigantic fish.

In order to escape, the sorcerer was forced to cast the most powerful spell at his command. Turning himself into a kernel of corn, he rolled into a tiny crack between two stones, out of the lad's reach. Instantly, the apprentice turned himself into a rooster. With his sharp beak, he dug out the tiny kernel and gobbled it up, putting an end to the wicked sorcerer.

The apprentice then became a full-fledged sorcerer. He took over the workshop, and from that day on used all his skills to make only good magic.

Red Riding Hood

THERE was once a sweet little maiden, who was loved by all who knew her; but she was especially dear to her Grandmother, who did not know how to make enough of the child. Once she gave her a little red velvet cloak. It was so becoming, and she liked it so much, that she would never wear anything else; and so she got the name of Red Riding Hood.

One day her Mother said to her: "Come here, Red Riding Hood, take this cake and bottle of wine to Grandmother; she is weak and ill, and it will do her good. Go quickly, and don't loiter by the way, or run, or you will fall down and break the bottle, and there will be no wine for Grandmother. When you get there, don't forget to say 'Good morning' prettily, without staring around you."

"I will do just as you tell me," Red Riding Hood promised her.

Her Grandmother lived away in the woods a good half-hour from the village. When she got to the wood, she met a Wolf; but Red Riding Hood did not know what a wicked animal he was, so she was not a bit afraid of him.

"Good morning, Red Riding Hood," he said.

"Good morning, Wolf," she answered.

"Where are you going so early, Red Riding Hood?"

"To Grandmother's."

"What have you got in your basket?"

"Cake and wine; we baked yesterday, so I'm taking a cake to Grannie; she needs something to make her well."

"Where does your Grandmother live, Red Riding Hood?"

"A good quarter of an hour further into the wood. Her house stands under three big oak trees, near a hedge of nut trees," said Red Riding Hood.

The Wolf thought: "This tender little creature will be a plump morsel; she will be nicer than the old woman. I must be cunning, and snap them both up."

He walked along with Red Riding Hood for a while, then he said: "Look at the pretty flowers, Red Riding Hood. Why don't you look around you? I don't believe you even hear the birds sing. You are just as solemn as if you were going to school; everything else is so gay out here in the woods."

Red Riding Hood raised her eyes, and when she saw the sunlight dancing through the trees, and all the bright flowers, she thought: "I'm sure Grannie would be pleased if I took her a bunch of fresh flowers. It is still quite early. I'll have plenty of time to pick them."

So she left the path, and wandered off among the trees to pick the flowers. Each time she picked one, she always saw another prettier one further on. So she went deeper and deeper into the forest.

In the meantime the Wolf went straight off to the Grandmother's cottage, and knocked at the door.

"Who is there?"

"Red Riding Hood, bringing you a cake and some wine. Open the door!"

"Press the latch!" cried the old woman. "I am too weak to get up."

The Wolf pressed the latch, and the door sprang open. He went straight in and up to the bed without saying a word, and ate up the poor old woman. Then he put on her nightgown and nightcap, got into bed and drew the curtains.

Red Riding Hood ran about picking flowers till she could carry no more, and then she remembered her Grandmother again. She was astonished when she got to the house to find the door open, and when she entered the room everything seemed so strange.

She felt frightened, but did not know why. "Generally I like coming to see Grandmother so much," she thought. She cried: "Good morning, Grandmother," but she received no answer.

Then she went up to the bed and drew the curtain back. There lay her Grandmother, but she had drawn her cap down over her face, and she looked very odd.

"Oh, Grandmother, what big ears you have got," she said.

"The better to hear with, my dear."

"Grandmother, what big eyes you have got."

"The better to see with, my dear."

"What big hands you have got, Grandmother."

"The better to catch hold of you with, my dear."

"But Grandmother, what big teeth you have got."

"The better to eat you with, my dear!"

And with that, the Wolf sprang out of bed, and devoured poor little Red Riding Hood. When the Wolf had satisfied himself, he went back to bed and was soon snoring loudly.

A Huntsman went past the house, and thought, "How loudly the old lady is snoring; I must see if there is anything the matter with her."

So he went into the house, and up to the bed, where he found the Wolf fast asleep. "Do I find you here, you old sinner?" he said. "I've been waiting to get my hands on you!"

He raised his gun to shoot, when it just occurred to him that perhaps the Wolf had eaten up the old lady, and that she might still be saved. So he took a knife and began cutting open the sleeping Wolf. At the first cut he saw the little red cloak, and after a few more slashes, the little girl sprang out, and cried: "Oh, how frightened I was, it was so dark inside the Wolf!" Next the old Grandmother came out, alive, but hardly able to breathe.

Red Riding Hood brought some big stones with which they filled the Wolf, so that when he woke and tried to spring away, they dragged him back, and he fell down dead.

They were all quite happy now. The Huntsman skinned the Wolf, and took the skin home. The Grandmother ate the cake and drank the wine which Red Riding Hood had brought, and she soon felt quite strong. Red Riding Hood thought: "I will never again wander off into the forest as long as I live, if my Mother forbids it." And she never did.

The Bremen Town Musicians

A FARMER lived near the town of Bremen. He had a donkey who had been a hard working animal, but now was growing weak with age. One day the old donkey was eating grass near the farm house.

"Old Hee-Haw is getting old," he heard the farmer say to his wife. "Tomorrow I'll take him to market and sell him to the tanner. With what he gives me for the skin, and a little more, I can buy a young donkey."

Poor old Hee-Haw began to shiver and shake. But suddenly he threw up his head. "Why should I be sold to the tanner?" he said to himself. "Age hasn't harmed my fine voice. In Bremen Town the people love music. I'll go there and earn my living as a musician."

Feeling much better, the old donkey trotted down the road to Bremen Town. After a while he stopped for a few bites of grass beside the road. Lying in the grass was a dog panting very hard.

"Why do you pant so, friend?" asked Hee-Haw. "And what is your name?"

"My name is Bruno," replied the dog. "For years I've guarded my master's house and his flocks, but now I'm old and my sight is not sharp enough for him. I overheard him telling his wife that he was going to knock me on the head and get a younger dog. So I ran away. But now I don't know where to go or how to earn my living."

"Can you still bark?" asked the donkey.

"Oh, yes," the dog replied. "Bow-wow-wow!"

"You have a fine deep note," said Hee-Haw. "Join me and go to Bremen Town. There we can make our living as musicians."

Up jumped the old dog, and side by side the two animals trotted toward Bremen Town. A little farther along they came to a place where a cat was sitting in the middle of the road, looking very sad.

"What is troubling you, master cat?" asked Hee-Haw.

"I'm homeless and hungry," said the cat. "For years I caught mice in my mistress's house; but now I can't move quickly enough, and the mice escape. I heard my mistress planning to tie a stone to my neck and drop me into the river. So I ran away. But now I don't know how to find a bite to eat."

"Can you still meow?" asked the donkey.

"Oh, yes indeed," replied the cat. "Me-ow!"

"That's a very sweet tone," said the donkey, "and should make excellent harmony with my bray and Bruno's bark. We are going to Bremen Town to earn our living as musicians. Won't you come with us?"

"Thank you," said the cat. "My name is Felix, and I shall be glad to meow with you."

Soon they passed a farmyard where a rooster was perched on top of the barn.

"Cock-a-doodle-do!" he crowed, flapping his wings.

"Why do you crow so loudly?" called the donkey.

"Because tomorrow will be a fine day," replied the rooster. "I always crow extra loud and long for fine weather. But it annoys my mistress. I just heard her tell the maid that she would wring my neck tomorrow and make soup of me."

"Then why not come with us?" suggested the donkey. "We are bound for Bremen Town to make our living as musicians."

"I'll go with pleasure," said the rooster. "My name is Chanticleer."

So they all went on toward Bremen Town.

Soon it began to grow dark and the donkey said they would have to spend the night in the woods. He and Bruno lay down under a tree. Felix climbed to one of the lower branches, and Chanticleer flew to the very top.

"There must be a house in the forest," he called down. "I see a light through the leaves."

"In that case," said Hee-Haw, getting up, "perhaps we can find more comfortable quarters than this rough ground. Where there's a house there's usually a barn."

They set off through the forest and in a few minutes came to the house.

"I'm the tallest," said Hee-Haw. "I'll go softly to the window and see what's inside."

He walked to the window and looked into the room. Then he walked back to the place where his friends were standing.

"I saw four robbers," he brayed, very softly. "On the table were piles of gold and jewels, and there were all sorts of good things to eat and drink."

"That would be a fine place for us to spend the night," growled Bruno, "if only we could get rid of the robbers."

"Robbers are easily frightened," purred Felix, "because they are not honourable."

"So they are," crowed Chanticleer, in a very small voice. "If, all together, we make as much noise as we can, perhaps we could frighten them away."

They all crept up to the window. Hee-Haw stood with his chin just above the sill. Bruno jumped on his back. Felix jumped on Bruno's back and Chanticleer flew up and perched on Felix's back.

"Now when I nod my head," said Hee-Haw, "let us, each one, make as much noise as possible."

Then, as Hee-Haw nodded: The donkey brayed, the dog barked, the cat meowed and the rooster crowed and flapped his wings.

"What in the world is that?" shouted one of the robbers, and all four sprang up from the table in great fear.

With a whir of his wings, Chanticleer flew in and put out the light. Felix came after him with a hiss. Bruno followed with a growl, and old Hee-Haw jumped through the window with a loud bray and a clatter of hoofs against the window frame.

The robbers were so frightened that they ran out of the house and didn't stop until they had put a full mile between themselves and the terrible noises that had come upon them so suddenly.

"The gold can wait," said Hee-Haw, sitting down at the table. "I'm hungry."

"So am I," said Bruno taking his place at the other end. Felix sat on one side and Chanticleer on the other side of the table, and when they got up again there was little left of the feast.

"Now," said the donkey, "I'm going to drag in a bunch of hay and lie here by the door."

"This thick rug will be my bed," said the dog.

"I'll sleep on the warm hearth," purred the cat.

"That rafter near the ceiling will make a perfect perch for me," crowed the rooster.

Meanwhile the robbers had run until they were tired out.

"What are we running away from, anyway?" asked one as they came to a stop.

"It must have been a troop of hobgoblins," said another.

"Yes, I never heard such horrible noises in all my life," said the third.

"Hobgoblins or no hobgoblins," said the fourth, "I'm going back for my gold and jewels."

The four robbers walked back through the forest. When they reached the house all was still and dark.

"I'll go in first," said the fourth robber, "and you all come close behind me."

He groped around until he found a candle.

"The fire's nearly out," he called, "but there are a few sparks that will be enough to light the candle."

He marched boldly to the fireplace, but what he took for sparks were the fiery eyes of Felix, glaring through the darkness. As he stooped, the cat sprang up with a hiss and buried her claws in his arm. The robber screamed and turned to run out of the door, but as he turned he stepped on Bruno's tail. The old dog growled and bit him in the leg. Then Chanticleer flew down and pecked his neck, and, as he came to the doorway, Hee-Haw kicked out with his hind legs and landed the robber on his back outside the door.

Terribly frightened they all ran away as fast as they could, and they never dared go back to the house again.

The four musicians settled down in comfort. With the gold and jewels the robbers had left they were able to buy all the food they needed, so they never went to Bremen Town after all.

But once a year, they give a concert for their own pleasure. They stand by the window as they did when they frightened the robbers, and as the donkey nods his head, all together they begin:

"Hee-haw! Hee-haw!" "Bow-wow! Bow-wow!"
"Me-ow! Me-ow!" "Cock-a-doodle-doo-oo-oo-oo!"

Snow-white and Rose-red

THERE once was a poor widow who lived in a lonely little cottage with a garden in front, where two rose-trees bloomed, one of which bore a white rose and the other a red. The widow had two children, who were like the rose-trees, for one was called Snow-white and the other Rose-red.

The two children loved each other so dearly that whenever they went out together they walked hand in hand. Very often they went out into the woods by themselves to pick berries, and the wild beasts would not harm them.

The children lived a very happy life with their dear mother in their pretty cottage home. In the evenings the mother would say, "Snow-white, bolt the door," and then they seated themselves round the hearth, and the mother put on her spectacles and read to them out of a favourite book, while the girls sat at their spinning wheels and listened.

One winter's evening, as they all sat comfortably together, someone knocked at the door as though he wished to be let in.

"Quick, Rose-red," said the mother, "open the door. Very likely some poor wanderer has come to seek shelter."

Rose-red ran to pull back the bolt and open the door, thinking to see a poor man, but instead, a great black bear pushed his head in and looked at them.

Rose-red screamed with fright, and Snow-white ran to hide herself behind her mother's bed.

But the bear told them not to be afraid, for he would not hurt them. "Please let me in. I am half frozen with the cold," he said, "and only wish to warm myself a little."

"Poor fellow," answered the mother; "lie down by the fire, but see that you do not burn your thick fur coat."

Then she called the children and told them to have no fear, for the bear would not harm them but was honest and respectable.

So Snow-white and Rose-red crept out from their hiding places and were not the least afraid of the bear, who asked the children to brush the snow from his fur for him. They fetched a broom and brushed the thick black coat till not a single flake remained, and then the bear stretched himself comfortably in front of the fire and growled gently with content.

Before long the children were quite at home with their clumsy guest, playing all sorts of tricks upon him. The bear seemed well pleased with this treatment, though, and when they became a little too rough, he would cry comically, "Please, children, don't kill me."

When bedtime came the mother told the bear that he might spend the night beside the hearth, and so be sheltered from the cold and storm.

As soon as morning dawned, the two children opened the door, and he trotted away across the snow and was lost to sight in the wood. But from that day on, the bear came to them every night at the same time, laid himself down beside the hearth, and let the children play pranks with him as they liked, and they soon grew so accustomed to him that they never thought of bolting the door until their friend had arrived.

When the spring came and the whole world was fresh and green, the bear told Snow-white one morning that he would not be able to visit them again all through the summer months.

"Where are you going, dear bear?" asked Snow-white.

"I must stay in the woods and guard my treasures from the wicked dwarfs. In the winter, when the ground is frozen hard, they cannot work their way through it and are obliged to stay below in their caves; but now that the warm sun has thawed the earth, they will soon break upward and come to steal what they can find, and that which once goes into their caves seldom comes out again."

Snow-white grieved sadly over the parting. As she unbolted the door and the bear hurried through, a piece of his coat caught on the latch and was torn off, and it seemed to the child that she saw a glimmer of gold beneath it, but she was not sure. The bear ran quickly away, and soon disappeared behind the trees.

Some time afterwards the mother sent the children into the woods to gather sticks. They came to a great tree that lay felled on the ground.

Beside it something very strange-looking kept jumping up and down in the grass.

At first they could not make out what it was, but as they came nearer they saw that it was a dwarf, with an old withered face and a long snow white beard. The end of his beard had been caught fast in a split in the tree, and the creature jumped about like a little dog at the end of a string and knew not how to help himself.

He glared at the little girls with his fiery red eyes and screamed, "Why do you stand staring there instead of coming to help me?"

"What have you been doing, little man?" asked Rose-red.

"You silly, prying goose," answered the dwarf; "if you *must* know, I was splitting the tree to get some small pieces of wood for the kitchen.

The large logs that you use would burn up our food in no time. We don't need to cook such a quantity as you great greedy folk. I had just driven the wedge firmly in and everything seemed right enough when it slipped on the smooth wood and popped out, so that the tree closed up in a second, catching my beautiful white beard as it did so; and now I cannot get it out again, and you foolish milk-faced creatures stand and laugh at me. Oh, how horrid you are!"

The children tried with all their might to help the old man, but they could not loosen his beard, and so Rose-red said she would run and fetch someone to help them.

"You stupid thing!" snarled the dwarf. "Why go and fetch others when you are two too many already? Can't you think of something better than that?"

"Have patience," said Snow-white. "I know what to do." And drawing her scissors from her pocket, she cut off the end of the old man's beard.

As soon as the dwarf was free he grabbed a bag of gold that was hidden among the roots of the tree, threw it across his shoulders, and grumbled out, "What clumsy folk, to be sure—to cut off a piece of my beautiful beard! Bad luck to you!" and then, without so much as a word of thanks to the children, away he went.

Some time afterwards Snow-white and Rose-red went to catch fish for dinner, and as they neared the brook, they saw something that looked like a grasshopper hopping along towards the water. They ran to it and soon recognized the dwarf.

"What *are* you doing?" said Rose-red; "surely you don't want to jump into the water?"

"I'm not quite such an idiot as that," shrieked the dwarf. "Can't you see that the horrid fish is pulling me in?"

The little man had been sitting fishing when the wind entangled his beard with the fishing line. Just at that moment a large fish took the bait and the little weak creature was not strong enough to pull it out.

So the fish had the upper hand and was drawing the dwarf towards it. It is true the dwarf clutched at the grass and rushes as he went along, but it was all in vain, and he was forced to follow every movement of the fish, so that he was in great danger of being dragged into the water.

The children came just at the right moment. They held the little man fast and tried to disentangle the line, but they could not do so, and at last there was nothing to do but to bring out the scissors and snip off a little piece of his beard.

The dwarf was very angry when he saw what they had done.

"Is it good manners," he yelled, "to spoil a person's face like that, you toads? Not content with having shortened my beard, you must cut the best part out of it. May you go barefoot all your days!"

Then he seized a bag of pearls that lay hidden in the reeds, marched off without another word, and disappeared behind a stone.

It happened that soon afterwards the mother sent her two little girls into town to buy needles and thread, and laces and ribbons. On their way home they again met the dwarf. He had emptied his sack of precious stones upon a smooth place, little thinking to be surprised by anyone at such a late hour. The evening sun shone upon the glistening heap of gems and made them sparkle and flash so prettily that the children stood still to look at them.

"Why do you stand gaping there?" screamed the dwarf, his ashen grey face crimson with wrath. He would have continued to scold but at that moment loud growls were heard, and a big black bear came shambling out of the wood.

In terror the dwarf sprang towards his cave, but the bear was too near, and he could not reach it. Then he cried in his despair, "Dear Mr. Bear, spare me, I pray you, and I will give you all my treasures. Look at these precious stones; they shall all be yours if only you will spare my life. I am such a little fellow you would scarcely feel me between your teeth, but here are these two wicked girls—take them and eat them; you will find them tender morsels, and as fat as young quails."

The bear took no heed of his words, but gave the wicked creature one stroke with his paw, and he never moved again.

The two little girls had begun to run away, but the bear now called to them, "Snow-white, Rose-red, do not be afraid. If you will wait for me, I will come with you."

They recognized his voice at once and stood still, and as the bear came up to them, his fur coat suddenly fell from him, and he stood there, a handsome young man, dressed all in shining gold.

"I am a King's son," he said, "and I was condemned by the wicked dwarf, who had stolen all my treasures, to become a bear and run wild in the woods until I should be released by his death. He has now received his well-earned reward."

When they grew up, the Prince married little Snow-white while Rose-red was betrothed to his brother, and they divided between them all the beautiful treasures that the dwarf had collected in his cave.

The poor old mother went to live with her dear children, and took with her the two rose-trees from her little garden. These she planted close to her window, and every year they were covered with the most beautiful red and white roses that ever were seen.

PRINTED IN BELGIUM BY
INTERNATIONAL BOOK PRODUCTION